THE

PIRATES

OF

CROCODILE

SWAMP

THE PIRATES OF CROCODILE SWAMP

BY **JIM ARNOSKY**

G. P. PUTNAM'S SONS

G. P. PUTNAM'S SONS
A division of Penguin Young Readers Group.
Published by The Penguin Group. Penguin Group (USA) Inc., 375 Hudson Street, New York,
NY 10014, U.S.A. Penguin Group (Canada), 90 Eglinton Avenue East, Suite 700, Toronto,
Ontario M4P 2Y3, Canada (a division of Pearson Penguin Canada Inc.). Penguin Books Ltd, 80
Strand, London WC2R 0RL, England. Penguin Ireland, 25 St. Stephen's Green, Dublin 2,
Ireland (a division of Penguin Books Ltd.). Penguin Group (Australia), 250 Camberwell Road,
Camberwell, Victoria 3124, Australia (a division of Pearson Australia Group Pty Ltd). Penguin
Books India Pvt Ltd, 11 Community Centre, Panchsheel Park, New Delhi - 110 017, India.
Penguin Group (NZ), 67 Apollo Drive, Rosedale, North Shore 0632, New Zealand (a division
of Pearson New Zealand Ltd). Penguin Books (South Africa) (Pty) Ltd, 24 Sturdee Avenue,
Rosebank, Johannesburg 2196, South Africa. Penguin Books Ltd, Registered Offices:
80 Strand, London WC2R 0RL, England.

Design by Richard Amari.
Text set in Cooper Oldstyle Light.
The art was done in Fine Tip Pilot Pen.

Library of Congress Cataloging-in-Publication Data
Arnosky, Jim. The pirates of Crocodile Swamp / Jim Arnosky. p. cm. Summary: Kidnapped by
their father, two boys escape into the mangrove swamps of Key Largo, Florida, where they learn
to live on their own among the wildlife. [1. Swamps—Fiction. 2. Animals—Florida—Fiction.
3. Brothers—Fiction. 4. Runaways—Fiction. 5. Survival—Fiction. 6. Family problems—Fiction.
7. Key Largo (Fla.)—Fiction.] I. Title. PZ7.A7384Pi 2009 [Fic]—dc22   2008009296

ISBN 978-0-399-25068-2
10 9 8 7 6 5 4 3 2 1

It was as if my whole life happened the way it did just to get me where I was—in a boat beside a tiny island in the freedom of the dark wild night.

THE

PIRATES

OF

CROCODILE

SWAMP

CHAPTER 1

WINTER 1982

The winter of 1982 was the worst ever, but not because of the cold. It was the winter my little brother Terry died. Terry was only four years old. I was eleven. My other brother Jack was nine. At Terry's funeral the sky was gray and spitting snow. He was buried in the big cemetery just outside Philadelphia in a plot with the other Casperins. They were all gone before I was born.

All the relatives I ever knew were Jack, Terry, Mom and Dad. Then we lost Terry.

Not too many people came to the burial. The only friends Dad had were just the other drinkers at Tony's Bar. Dad always said Tony was his best friend, but Tony didn't show up for Terry. Mom had a handful of friends from where she used to work. They all made it to Terry's tiny gravesite, standing uncomfortably on the frozen ground, with snow flurries sticking to their tearstained faces.

Terry didn't have a priest to pray over him. We weren't churchgoers. The funeral director said some prayers, the same prayers he said over everybody, no matter who they were or how old they were. I said a prayer to Terry telling him not to be afraid, that there were lots of little kids in heaven and he'd make friends. I heard Mom praying too. But mostly she cried. Dad didn't cry. He just stared at the tiny casket. And when he wasn't staring at Terry's casket, he was staring at me and Jack with a mean look in his eyes. We knew what that look meant. It meant we had better keep our mouths shut about what really happened: Terry didn't accidentally fall by himself down the living room stairs like we all said he did.

Our family never worked right because of Dad's drinking. Whatever it was that made him drink, we never knew. All we knew was that when he drank, he got angry, and when he got angry, he took it out on us.

My mom's name was Rose. She dealt with Dad's drinking by pretending everything was rosy and that there was really nothing wrong. Secretly she prayed for things to get better. But they never did.

Jack's real name was John, after Dad. He preferred Jack, though, because it went better with the word *jungle*. He called himself Jungle Jack. Jack watched every wildlife show he could find on TV. All he cared about were wild animals and the wild places where they lived. He always said he was going to run away someday and live in the jungle.

My name is Sandy. I was Mr. Responsible. I took care of Mom when she had been crying. I brought food from the school cafeteria when there wasn't any at home because Dad spent his whole paycheck in Tony's Bar. I found library books for Jack so he could read about the animals he watched on TV. Jack didn't like going into the library. He said it was too quiet and gave him the "geebees." The last time he was in our school library he stood on a table and pounded his chest like a gorilla. So I got books for him. It kept him out of trouble.

I looked after Terry too, for as long as I could. He was a great little guy. Every day he discovered something new. He'd watch the sun gradually brighten through the window blinds as if it were a show being put on especially for him. Terry was the happiest part of our lives. And his death was the final blow to our family.

I tried to erase Terry's death from my brain by not talking about him; by telling myself that it was just an accident. Which is what it was, except that it was an accident that never should have happened.

The day Terry died, Dad had come home early from work, drunker than ever. He staggered in, threw his jacket on the floor and headed up the stairs, bumping his shoulder against the wall as he made each step. Mom found the empty whiskey bottle in his coat pocket. She ran to the foot of the stairs, shaking the bottle in the air and screaming up at him.

"You see this?" Her voice was trembling with hurt and anger. "Can you see how this is killing you? It's killing all of us!"

Jack and I watched the whole thing from the living room. I can still see Dad standing wobbly at the top of the stairs, cursing and mumbling that we were bleeding him dry. We were chains around his legs, and he was tired of working all day long to feed our grubby faces. Then Terry came out of his bedroom holding his stuffed bear and walked silently over to Dad's side. But Dad didn't see Terry. He was too busy ranting. He pulled off his belt to threaten us with it and, swinging his arm, accidentally hit Terry.

Dad knocked Terry down the stairs. Not on purpose. But he did, and that's what killed my brother. It's why Dad stayed out later and later every night and came home drunker and meaner each time. And it was Terry's death that made Mom feel so low, she stopped praying for things to get better. She just sat like a wilted flower in front of the TV as if that stupid screen was the sun. She didn't look right at us anymore. If you asked her something, she would answer you—but she'd never look away from the TV, its light flickering in her eyes.

Eventually Mom stopped talking to us completely. She talked, but not to us. She just repeated the whole thing about Dad knocking Terry down the stairs. "He killed my baby boy," she said over and over.

Dad shouted at her to make her stop. "Shut up! Shut up, I tell you!" We could see how guilty he felt. "Rose. Please. Stop it!"

And when she wouldn't listen, he'd go wild, pushing over chairs and clearing pictures and lamps off tables with a sweep of his hand, all the while yelling at Mom. "Stop it! Shut up! *Shut up!*"

But Mom wouldn't shut up. She kept repeating herself, not once looking away from the TV. It drove Dad nuts! It was making us all crazy. It went on and on, day after day. We didn't know how long Dad could stand it.

One day, we were getting on the school bus to go home when Dad's big gray Chevy pulled up. That was a surprise; Dad never picked us up from school. We ran to the car and crawled in the backseat, expecting a ride home. But we didn't go home. Instead, we headed out of town. Jack spotted a bandage on Dad's right hand with some blood seeping through over the knuckles. He jumped forward and blurted out, "Where's Mom?"

Dad reached with his bandaged hand and shoved Jack back in his seat.

"Never mind about Mom!" Dad said. "She's not coming with us!"

Right then I knew Dad was running, leaving Mom for good. Why he was taking us, I couldn't figure. Then it occurred to me: he didn't want us to see Mom! Suddenly I felt all sick inside thinking about what could have happened back home.

We drove all night. We didn't even stop to eat. We only stopped for gas, to use the restroom and for something to drink. Dad drank a lot of coffee. Jack got drowsy and fell asleep, but I couldn't. I sat staring out my window, watching the dark shapes of trees go by. We left Mom in Pennsylvania and kept traveling south on I-95. Dad was sober and tense.

"I'm hungry!" Jack complained, half asleep.

But Dad didn't respond. He just steered straight ahead on the dark road. I stayed awake all the way through Baltimore and Washington, D.C. Then I fell asleep.

My brother and I were conked out for a good twelve hours. We would have slept longer if Dad hadn't dozed off and swerved momentarily out of his lane. An oncoming truck blasted its horn and woke us all up, just in time for Dad to avoid a crash. We were barreling down the highway at 80 mph.

The morning sun was warm through the windows and it felt hot on my legs and arms. There were tall palm trees on the sides of the road. I looked at Jack. He was reading a passing billboard aloud.

DAYTONA BEACH SURF SHOP

We were in Florida!

Dad drove all morning, still going south on Interstate 95. Around noon, we finally stopped to eat. We were starved. After that Dad got a second wind. He started passing trucks and campers with a vengeance. He had his wallet on the passenger seat. I watched him steer with one hand and go through his wallet with the other, checking his cash. It didn't look like much. I wondered how he planned to pay for all our food and a place for us to stay. He couldn't use his credit cards if he was on the run. And he was on the run, all right! Looking back on it, I don't think he had any plan. He was just running, and he kept on running all the way down I-95 until it ended. Then he picked up U.S. Route 1 and drove south on it. No, Dad didn't have a plan. He was just escaping from whatever it was he was afraid of back home.

U.S. 1 crossed over a small bridge and the land on the other side narrowed until it was not much wider than the highway. We were surrounded by water. We passed a road sign that read

WELCOME TO THE FLORIDA KEYS

and Dad finally slowed down.

Jack and I sat up in our seats. There was blue-green water everywhere we looked and dozens of tiny dark green islands. Big, white, long-legged birds were wading near the shore. Others were perched on the island trees.

"Egrets," Jack said low to himself. He had seen these birds before on TV.

The sun was going down over the water. As it sank below the horizon, the big orange globe appeared to stretch wide and flatten, then shrink before winking out of sight. I looked at Jack, who was still staring out at the sundown scene. His mouth was turned up in a small smile. He saw beauty outside. I saw it too, but I didn't feel like smiling.

*I*t was dark out when Dad pulled into the Key Largo Motel. There were two palm trees at the entrance, each wrapped from the ground up with white lights. It looked like a happy place. Jack and I stayed in the car with Jack's window down. The motel's office door was wide open. We heard Dad check in as John Jones instead of John Casperin. He paid cash for the room.

"I wonder if we're gonna be Joneses too?" Jack whispered to me.

Dad was tired. He walked stiff-legged and sore from the long drive. When we were in the room, he took off his shoes, turned on the TV and stretched out on one of the twin beds; and in less than five minutes he was out. And I mean out!

Jack and I watched him for a while to see if he'd move. His big chest rose and fell in deep sleep breathing, but the rest of him was dead to the world. His right hand hung down off the bed. The bandage wrapped around his hand had worn at the edges, showing part of the bruises on his knuckles. The blood on the bandage was dry and brown.

"Let's get outta here!" Jack whispered.

"Wait!" I told him. "We don't even know where we are, and it's dark outside. If we don't know where to go, or where we can hide, he'll find us and drag us back here. We're not going anywhere 'til morning, when we can see our way around."

Jack picked up the TV remote, plopped down

on our bed and started changing the channels with the sound real low. Staring at the TV screen reminded me of Mom and I wondered how she was.

"Do you think Mom's still sitting and staring at the TV right now?" I asked Jack. "You think she even knows we're gone?"

"I don't think she knows anything. I think she's dead," he replied.

"Dead?!"

"Yeah, dead! Do you think we'd be hidin' out here in Florida with *Mr. Jones* if Mom was alive?"

Leave it to Jack to come up with the worst possible scenario. I knew Dad must have done something awful to make him run so far from home, but no way did I think he killed Mom.

"Get real, Sandy! Look at his hand! He hit Mom with it! You know how he is." Jack lowered his voice to below a whisper. "Mom was mumblin' that stuff about Terry and Dad finally blew his top. He hit her and knocked her down, like he did Terry."

There was a phone on the night table near our bed. I lifted the receiver and listened for a dial tone.

"What are you doin'?" Jack asked, shooting a look at Dad.

"I'm gonna call Mom and see . . . "

"See what?"

"If she's okay."

"She's not okay! You know she isn't. Besides, even if she's not dead and just sittin' there starin' at the TV like she has been, she's not gonna answer the phone. When was the last time we saw her get up and answer the phone? She'll just let it ring. You know that! She'll ignore it, the way she ignored us."

Jack was probably right. But I thought Mom would answer if she could. Even so, I put the motel phone back down as quietly as I could. I was starting to feel queasy, like I was going to gag. I swallowed hard and said, "Jack, we're in trouble here!"

"Trouble? We're not in trouble. *He's* in trouble.

All we gotta do is get outta here and find the cops. We'll tell them about Dad and they'll put him in jail."

"But what if Dad didn't do anything to be arrested for?" I asked. "What if he did and they *do* arrest him, Jack? What happens to us?"

Jack looked at me for a long time, thinking about what I said. He was figuring things out. Finally he spoke.

"We can't go home. Whether Mom's dead or not, she won't be able to take care of us. The cops wouldn't let us stay by ourselves. And Mom and Dad's all the family we got."

"Right, Jack. They'll put us in some home. They may even have to split us up." Just saying it put the brakes on my brain. I went numb all over. Jack turned white and empty-looking.

"We can't tell on him," he said slowly to himself. "We can't tell anybody about Mom. We can't even ask anybody for help."

"We gotta ditch Dad. That's for sure," I told

Jack. "But after that, it's just you and me. On our own."

Both of us sat on the bed staring at some dumb doctor show on TV. Jack started changing channels again and something caught my eye.

"Stop. Go back!" I said a little too loud.

Jack hushed me and began switching back channel after channel.

"Stop!" I said again, only much softer. "That's the one."

It was a local channel advertising the different places in the area.

"This is just a bunch of commercials," Jack said, aiming the remote at the screen again. "I wanna find a wildlife show."

"No, Jack! Look! Listen to this stuff!"

The channel was showing an aerial view of the long string of islands called the Keys. The narrator said that the Florida Keys were connected by a single road, U.S. 1, which ran 120 miles from Key Largo to Key West. Every place you wanted to find in the Keys was found by its mile marker. The closer to Key West you went, the lower the mile marker number.

"I think I saw one of those marker things just as we were pulling in here!" Jack said. "It was a small green sign with the number 102 on it."

He picked up the tourist booklet on the night table and leafed through until he found a map.

"Here we are!" Jack whispered to me.

I moved closer on the bed to see and it made a loud springy noise. Dad rolled over on his side toward us. He groaned, but his eyes stayed shut. He was still out like a light. Jack ran his finger on the map to show me Route 1. He pointed to mile marker 102.

"See? We're right here, smack in the middle of Key Largo."

We studied the map together. It was like discovering a whole new world. Each time the guy on the Keys channel mentioned a new place, we located the mile marker on our map. When the guy said the water on one side of the Keys was a shallow bay, we put our fingers on the blue color of Florida Bay. When the narrator talked about the other side of the Keys being the ocean side, we moved our fingers over to the Atlantic Ocean on the map. I noticed that in Key Largo, Route 1 ran very close to the bay; and since we'd seen water on the way in, I told Jack that we were probably on the bay side of the Keys.

Just then the Keys channel began a story about a wild place in Key Largo called Crocodile Swamp. Jack's eyeballs nearly popped out of his head! The TV showed real live crocodiles swimming around little trees called mangroves that grew up out of the water. The swamp in Key Largo was one of the last strongholds of the North American crocodile. The whole swamp was off-limits to the public.

"Let's go there!" Jack said. "Nobody's allowed in. No one will ever find us there."

I looked at the map again and searched for Crocodile Swamp. There it was! It was only about five miles away from our motel, but I wasn't sure I should tell Jack. I rolled the booklet up and held it to hide the map from him. I wasn't too keen on going into a place full of crocodiles. Jack's eyes were glued to the TV, watching crocodile after crocodile slide into the waters of Crocodile Swamp. Some of them looked big enough to bite a person's head off. I tried to get Jack's attention.

"Awesome," he said to himself. He didn't hear me at all.

It was no use. Jack was in his jungle trance. I waited until the channel finished its story about the crocodiles. Then I explained, "Jack, those are real crocodiles in Crocodile Swamp. Crocodiles that can eat people."

"We don't have to get close to any," Jack said. "We'll keep our distance from them. But havin' them in there would sure keep Dad from going in. He'll never even look for us in Crocodile Swamp!"

Jack was right about that—no one would look for us in a crocodile-infested swamp. I unrolled the booklet and showed him where Crocodile Swamp was on the map.

"As soon as it gets light out, we'll make a break for it," I said. "You go through his stuff and get his money. We'll need some money."

Jack eyeballed Dad's wallet on the table near his bed and smiled. He liked the idea of robbing Dad.

We watched the Keys channel programs over and over. Whether we got to Crocodile Swamp or not, the more we learned about the Keys, the better chance we had to stay one step ahead of Dad. He was going to be madder than ever. I found a pen in our table drawer and circled Crocodile Swamp on the map. Then I tucked the booklet in my back pocket. The clock on the table said three A.M.

At four it was still dark outside, but I could see the shapes of the tall palm trees at the motel entrance. Jack was dozing off. I wasn't tired. I sat staring at Dad. He and I were look-alikes. We had the same shape chins and noses. We both had gray eyes and sandy-colored hair. I feared I would be like him in other ways. Most of the time he was cursing and bothered by something or somebody. And he always seemed nervous and agitated, always looking over his shoulder, like he was expecting a fight. It was hard to figure. His drinking made him worse. It made him lash out, usually at us. He hit us all the time.

When the TV began running the story about Crocodile Swamp for the fifth or sixth time, Jack woke up, and we watched it again. It was then we realized the swamp was accessible only by boat. We hadn't caught that before.

"We don't have a boat," I said.

Jack snuck around Dad's bed, passing his big shoeless feet. He went to Dad's night table and lifted Dad's wallet. There were some ones and fives. But hidden inside, under a leather flap, Jack found a bunch of fifties and twenties. He held the

wad of bills up and said in a low whisper, "We'll
buy a boat!"

Suddenly, Dad sat up, rubbing the palm of his
injured hand against his eyes.

"Wha . . . What time is—Hey! What are you
doing?!"

Jack jumped away, the money still in his hand.
Dad lunged, trying to grab Jack as he passed the
foot of the bed.

I kicked Dad's shoes across the room and then
ran to open the door. Jack knocked over a chair
to block Dad's way, and then we both took off
across the parking lot.

In his stocking feet, Dad hit the lot's crushed
shells and let out a yell. We looked back and saw
him running clumsily. He smashed his right foot
against a cement curb and went down, moaning
in pain.

"Come back here! You . . . I'll get you! I'll find
you both! You're gonna pay for this . . . Owww!"

Dad rolled over, trying to get up. Jack yelled
back, "You'll have to catch us first!"

It felt good just to be running hard and feeling my legs pumping after being cooped up for so long. We ran through a gas station where cars towing boats were filling their tanks. We passed a pier where fishermen were loading a big boat with coolers and tackle boxes. I was way ahead of Jack. I was older and taller than him, and had a long stride, but I ran and ran and never looked back. I booked it out onto Route 1 and ran along the shoulder of the busy highway, sucking in deep drafts of exhaust fumes mingled with salt air.

Up ahead was a huge statue of a tropical fish. I flew toward it, barely feeling the soles of my feet hitting the ground. When I got to the fish I stopped and turned around, expecting to see Jack right behind me. But Jack wasn't there. I stared down the highway; no Jack.

The sky was lightening as the sun began to come up over the trees and still no Jack.

I bet he didn't run fast enough, I thought. Then I said out loud, "I bet he tripped and fell right out in the open on Route 1 where Dad could see him, and he got nabbed."

"No he didn't!" said a voice from above.

It was Jack, on top of the big fish! How he got there without me seeing him, I'll never know. He pounced down on me like a cat and knocked us both to the ground. We wrestled and rolled and laughed so hard, it hurt my empty stomach.

"I'm gonna pee!" Jack yelled, laughing and rolling toward me.

"Don't pee on me!" I shouted, pushing him away.

It was a bright morning of a brand-new day, and it felt good being free.

CHAPTER 3
LIBERTAD

Jack and I lay awhile on the ground just staring up at the cloudless sky. As we were getting up, I saw Dad's Chevy coming. Its dull gray primer paint made it easy to spot. It looked like a big shark cruising down the highway. I grabbed Jack's shirt and pulled him behind the statue. Together we watched the car go by with Dad inside looking left and right, hunting for us.

"We better not stay out in the open," I said,

watching the tail end of the Chevy going away.

"Look," Jack said. "There's a lot of people down there. We can hide in the crowd."

Behind the big fish statue there were rows and rows of small storage sheds. Cars and trucks were pulling up and one by one the shed doors were being opened. Inside each little shed was a tiny store with tables covered with junk and all kinds of stuff hanging on the walls. Early morning bargain hunters were already crowding in to shop.

"It's a flea market," I said to Jack.

"We oughtta do some shopping," Jack said. "If we're gonna go to Crocodile Swamp, we'll need supplies." He counted Dad's money—two hundred and fifty dollars! We were rich!

The group of sheds was much more than a flea market. Each shed store was different from the next. One sold boat anchors and propellers and brass bells and wooden models of sailing ships. Another was packed solid with all kinds of dolls. Jack and I went into a shed filled with fishing equipment. For less than twenty dollars, we bought a used spinning rod with a reel full of seventeen-pound test line, and a small plastic tackle box loaded with bobbers, sinkers, hooks and lures. Under all the tackle was a filet knife. Jack unsheathed the knife and lightly ran his thumb along the blade. It was sharp.

I asked the guy selling us the stuff if the line was strong enough to catch big fish. He said we could catch a whale on that seventeen-pound test line, as long as we had the drag set right. He showed us where the knob was on the reel that you turn to set the drag.

"You just set that drag so's it will give out line when a big fish tugs too hard," he explained, licking at the big gap in his mouth where his front teeth used to be. "As long as you're giving line, a fish can't bust it, no matter how big he is . . . unless of course he's got sharp teeth. Sharp teeth will cut through any strength line."

In another shed, Jack handed me a tiny kerosene camp stove, saying, "We can cook on this without making a smoky fire."

I was impressed! Jack was really thinking this Crocodile Swamp thing through. We bought the stove and a pint of kerosene to go with it for only five bucks. Almost everything was affordable. We bought a couple of used snorkel masks, an aluminum frying pan and a book on Florida fish. But the one thing we needed most—a boat—was way out of our price range. Even a small inflatable boat cost over three hundred dollars. I said we'd keep looking.

We spent the whole morning in the market amid the happy sounds of people buying and selling and joking around. We didn't even know these people, but they all took time to talk to us and wish us a nice day and tell us about the things we were buying from them.

The flea market people were not only interesting to listen to, they were fun to look at! The woman who sold us a silver camping blanket that folded up neatly into a tiny pouch had a black ponytail that reached all the way down to the ground! We bought an old beat-up pair of binoculars from a guy who had a gray ponytail almost as long as the woman's, and he had a tattoo of a tarantula on his arm. Everybody had tattoos! We saw a woman in short shorts with tattoos of snakes crawling up her legs. And there was a tattoo of a life-size fly on the nose of the man who helped us pick out a map of the Keys that had Crocodile Swamp in detail on it. We bought the map, a flashlight, an eight-pack of batteries, and a huge five-gallon plastic bucket to carry most of our stuff in for fifteen dollars.

A horn honked and the crowd made way for an old dilapidated truck, all decked out to look like a pirate ship. The driver of the truck was dressed like Captain Hook and he raised his plastic-hooked hand to wave at everyone he passed.

"Arrgh!" he growled.

"Aye, aye, Cap'n," I said as he went by. That's when Jack grabbed my arm and squeezed hard.

"He's here!" Jack said.

"Who?"

"Dad! There, behind the pirate truck!"

I saw him, limping along like a real peg-legged pirate. His was the only face in the crowd that wasn't smiling. We didn't wait around for him to see us. Jack and I each grabbed the handle of our bucket full of stuff and took off running as fast as we could through the maze of people and parked cars, all the way to the beach behind the sheds. And we didn't stop there. We kept on running along the shore, splashing on the wet sand until we were both out of steam. Jack let go of the bucket and plopped hands down on a boulder at the water's edge. I just crouched where I stopped.

"He didn't see us," Jack wheezed.

"That . . . was . . . too . . . close!" I said, trying to catch my breath.

"We were lucky," Jack said. "He coulda been right behind us. He coulda grabbed us both without having to run after us!"

"We gotta be more careful in crowded places," I told him. "We can't get taken by surprise like that."

"There won't be crowds in Crocodile Swamp, Sandy. We'll be alone there. We'll be safe there."

Crocodile Swamp was sounding better and better the longer we were on our own. But how we were going to get there was anybody's guess. Meanwhile, Jack was still going on about our close call.

"Did you see him limping on his sore foot? He looked mean. He looked like he could kill somebody. I hate him! I hate his guts!"

It was lunchtime and we hadn't eaten. A little ways down the shore there was a boat dock and deck with umbrellas and tables and people eating outside. We checked our cash. Jack showed me a handful of bills and some change. We still had almost two hundred dollars left! He gave me half of the money and jammed his half back in his pocket. He slapped me a high five and said, "Race you to the dock, *dork*!" Then he took off, leaving me to carry our bucket of gear. Even so, we reached the dock and restaurant together.

Jack picked a table at the very end of the deck and sat where he could see up and down the shoreline and all the water in that part of the bay. I sat facing the restaurant and the parking lot so I could be on the lookout for Dad's gray Chevy.

"Sandy. See those trees way out in the water? Those are mangroves. They only grow in tropical places."

"Huh?" I was still watching the parking lot.

"See how they stand up on their roots? That's how you tell."

I turned to Jack. "Tell what?"

"Tell that they're mangroves!"

"Can I help you?" A girl's voice made me turn and look. It was the waitress. She looked about my age—too young to be a waitress. She had short brown hair with yellow streaks in front. Her face was tanned and she had three earrings in each ear and rings on all ten fingers. She was holding a pad and pencil, ready to write our order.

"My name is Mia. I'm your server. Can I help you?"

"Uh, yeah," I stammered, and picked the first
thing I saw on the menu. "Fish and chips. I'll have
some fish and chips."

"Gimme fishin' chips too!" Jack said.

"Okay," Mia said, smiling at Jack. Then she
walked away.

Jack hopped his chair closer to me.

"Hey, Sandy, what's fishin' chips?"

I didn't answer because I didn't know. I turned to watch the parking lot again.

"We gotta be careful here," I said to Jack without looking at him. "The highway's awful close."

"If we see him, we run! That's all," Jack replied. "We're faster than him. He can't catch us. Besides, he won't last long down here. He hasn't got any money." He pulled out his wad of Dad's bills and, waving them, said slyly, "Remember?"

But I knew better. Dad must have had more money. In the car, maybe in the glove compartment. He must have gotten together more than two hundred and fifty dollars—three hundred counting the money he paid for the motel room—to make his getaway. Most likely he took Mom's wedding band and diamond engagement ring. It wouldn't be the first time he hocked them to get some quick cash. He always got them back, but it hurt Mom every time she had to give them up.

Before long, Mia returned with two baskets, each one stacked high with french fries and pieces of deep-fried fish. The food smelled great.

She put one basket in front of me and one in front of Jack. Watching her walk, I saw she also had silver rings on two of her toes.

Mia pulled a bottle out of her apron.

"Ketchup?" she asked.

"Yep," Jack said, already munching fries.

"Thank you," I said. She smiled at me this time.

"You look too young to work in a restaurant," Jack said with his mouth all red with ketchup. I kicked him under the table.

"My folks own the place," Mia said, "and they let me serve tables on weekends. It's fun and I make a little money. And it helps them out. Where are you two from?"

"Up north," Jack said. "How old are you, anyway?"

"I'm twelve," Mia told him politely. "How old are you?"

"I'm nine and he's—"

"Twelve!" I said loudly.

"He's eleven." Jack laughed, spitting bits of fish on the table.

"And a half!" I added, wanting to choke my little brother right there. "My name is Sandy."

"Nice to meet you, Sandy. And who's your friend?"

I looked at Jack and said, "Oh! He's not my friend. He's my brother . . . "

"*Jack!*" Jack butted in.

"Hi, Jack!" Mia chuckled.

Somebody spotted a dolphin in the bay and everyone on the deck looked out at the water. That's when I noticed the old boat lying on its side at the water's edge. It looked as if it had just washed up on shore.

"Whose boat is that?" I asked Mia.

"That's a Cuban freedom boat."

"A freedom boat?" Jack and I said the words together.

"That's right," Mia told us. "Cuba's an island, ninety or one hundred miles away. The Cuban people aren't free to leave their country and come here. Those that want to badly enough sneak away and float here on homemade boats."

"One hundred miles is a long way to float!" I said.

"That boat came all the way from Cuba last year," Mia said. "A man, a woman and their little girl were in it. When the Coast Guard found them, they just left the boat floating. Daddy found it one day when he was fishing and brought it here as a curiosity for our customers."

"So the boat belongs to your father?" I asked.

"I guess so," Mia answered. "But Daddy says a freedom boat can't belong to anyone except those it carries to freedom. That boat says so right on the side. See? *Libertad*. That's Spanish for freedom. Enjoy your meal."

I squinted to see the name on the boat.

"L-I-B-E-R-T-A-D. *Libertad*," I read aloud.

Jack gave me the thumbs-up and said, "Freedom!"

We didn't say another word while we ate. I

forgot all about watching the parking lot for Dad's Chevy. All I could think about was the little boat and Crocodile Swamp. Jack gobbled down his fish and chips like he was in a food-eating contest. All the while he ate, his eyes stayed glued to the *Libertad* down on the beach. He stuffed his last three or four french fries into his mouth all at once, stood up chewing way too much food and said, "I'm dub! I'm gobba go wooka daboat!"

While Jack went down to the boat, I stayed to pay our bill. I counted out the amount and added a tip for Mia. Then I jammed the rest of the money back in my pocket, grabbed our supplies and ran down to check out the freedom boat with Jack.

Up close, the boat didn't look so small. Jack walked off the length and width—twelve feet by five feet. The outside was covered with layers of varnished canvas stretched tight over a wooden frame. There was one plywood seat right in the center. The sides of the boat were high—nearly up to my belly. And cut into the top of each side was a deep notch. I figured the notches were for holding the oars in place when the boat was being rowed. Inside, on a floor made out of flattened kerosene cans, there were two long handmade oars and something else long, all wrapped up in a large cloth made up of a colorful patchwork of smaller cloths.

"I bet that's a mast and sail," I guessed.

The edges of the sail were neatly tucked and sewn by hand. I imagined the Cuban woman sewing in secret, dreaming of freedom for her and her family, but worrying about the long boat trip. That's how I was feeling too.

The beach was deserted. Jack looked up at the people on the deck, to be sure none of them was watching. Then he went to the front of the boat and tried to lift it, but it was too heavy. I laughed at the way his face got all red and his veins bulged out of his neck. We tried lifting the boat together. It was heavy but we raised it a good two inches off the beach, enough to know we could drag it into the water if we wanted to. We held the boat and looked at each other, laughing at both our red faces. Then we gently lowered the boat back down on the sand.

Jack claimed it: "Ours!"

I grabbed our map so we could plan our trip with it and put the bucket with the rest of our new gear in the boat and covered it with a part of the patchwork sail.

"We'll come back tonight and take the boat," I said. And Jack gave me another thumbs-up.

We spent the afternoon on a small beach not too far from the *Libertad*. The beach was nice and sandy and hidden by mangroves. Jack rolled the map out flat on the sand. I put a small seashell on the spot where I thought the boat was beached. Jack put his finger on the area marked Crocodile Swamp. It was a long way for us to row.

"Jeesh," Jack said, "we'll never get there to-night."

"We don't have to," I told him. "All we have to do tonight is cross the water to this little island. The island's right on the other side of a channel." I pointed on the map to the island and the channel. "The map shows that the channel is marked out in the water with a sign."

"We'll look for the sign," Jack agreed.

Planning the voyage on paper was easy, actually making it would be something else. I sat on the sand with my knees pulled up under my chin and looked out across the water. What was out there? What could be swimming under the boat as we rowed? What sort of danger would be just a few layers of varnished canvas away from Jack and me? Then I thought of Dad and Mom and Terry and the whole rotten mess. Jack and I would never go back! Even if we had to fight off crocodiles for the rest of our lives.

"Hey Sandy!"

I looked at Jack. He had a long strand of seaweed hanging out of each nostril. He smiled a big dumb smile. There was another piece of seaweed in his mouth, blacking out his two front teeth. We both cracked up.

Route 1 wasn't far away. We could hear the traffic going by. Jack and I found a path up to the highway and looked around. It was late in the afternoon and we were hungry again. There was an Arby's down the highway, right next to the entrance to a Kmart. We ate our last shore meal at Arby's, then went to Kmart to pick up a few more supplies—a small first-aid kit, mosquito netting, a couple of floating boat cushions for life preservers, two thick candles, waterproof matches, a box of Cheerios, a bag of dried fruit, a dozen cans of sardines for food and a jar of dead minnows for bait. We also bought a small bottle of cooking oil for any fish we caught.

While I was waiting in line to pay, Jack ran and grabbed us a couple of toothbrushes, a tube of toothpaste, a pack of fine-tip black markers and a small notepad to write on. When I saw the toothbrushes, I rubbed my fingers on my teeth. They were gross! I hadn't brushed them in two whole days!

We left Kmart as the sun was going down. By the time we reached the hidden beach, it was twilight. We were close enough to the restaurant to see the outdoor deck lights go on and hear the sounds of people at the tables. Someone was playing a guitar and singing. It sounded like everyone was having fun. Jack and I settled down on the beach and waited.

Jack must have been having second thoughts about our trip because he asked me, "What about crocs?"

"What about them?"

"Are you afraid of them?"

"No," I lied. "You?"

"Naah!"

The people and music at the restaurant's outdoor tables got louder. Jack passed the time playing with a little crab he had caught. He let it walk in his hand and up his arm. He let it go and caught it again. The sky got darker and darker and the water in the bay turned from blue-green to black. I stared at the dark water listening to the music down the beach and thought about how Mom used to sing while she ironed clothes or washed dishes. Before Terry died, when Dad wasn't drinking or when he wasn't around, Mom was happy, just like the people singing and eating on the restaurant deck. Seeing Mom happy always made me feel happy too.

The lights on the restaurant's crowded deck brightened the beach all the way down to the water. I could see the bow of the *Libertad* shining. When the guitar music stopped, the people began to leave. Soon afterward, the outdoor deck lights went out. Jack finally released the crab. It was time to make our move.

When we got down to the boat, Jack lifted a coil of old rope in the bow and discovered a big empty plastic jug with a few drops of water left in it. He suddenly remembered something he had seen on TV.

"Salt water!" he blurted out. "Crocodiles live in salt water. Crocodile Swamp is all salt water! We'll need freshwater to drink."

There was a hose hanging on the restaurant dock. I ran to it, turned the spigot on and stretched the long hose down to the boat. Jack held the jug while I filled it to the top. We each took a long drink of the running water, then recoiled the hose and put it back on the dock just as it had been. Jack found a small anchor with line on the beach close to the boat. He put them in the *Libertad* next to where I stashed our groceries. Then, lifting the bow together, we slowly pushed the boat into the water, and climbed in.

"No leaks!" Jack said as he fitted an oar into his side of the boat. I did the same on my side, and after a little clumsy oar dragging near shore, we got the hang of it and rowed out into the bay.

During the day the water was so clear, you could see the bottom sand a distance from the beach. At night the water was as black as the sky. Jack and I rowed in the darkness, pulling on our oars at the exact same time to keep the boat going straight. We couldn't see where we were going. We were sitting backward in the boat in order to row. Even when we twisted around to look over the bow, we couldn't see anything but blackness. We rowed and rowed and the *Libertad* glided along in the dark.

The air was dead still. The only sounds were the squeaking of the oars, the scrape of our shoes against the floor and the tiny splashes the oars made in the water.

Jack spotted a twinkling white light back on shore. I saw it too.

"They're coming!" Jack said, and he pulled harder on his oar, making the boat turn the wrong way.

"Who's coming?"

"The owners of the boat! They're coming after us! That's them on shore with a flashlight!"

"Jack. It's late. The restaurant's closed. No-body's even gonna know the boat's missing until tomorrow morning."

Jack was tense. I held his arm to keep him from rowing us around in a circle. The light on shore got brighter and brighter and Jack got more and more nervous. Then the light got higher and higher. It wasn't a flashlight. It was the moon rising over Key Largo! Once it was above the tree line, it hung there like a giant lightbulb in the night sky.

Jack's face brightened in the moonlight. He smiled to himself. We started rowing again and every ripple and wave the oars made in the water shone white with moonlight. The *Libertad*'s wake glowed like a long white road back toward shore. Watching the shining trail gave us a good idea of how far we had rowed.

We were about halfway across the bay when something splashed near Jack's oar. Then a great bulge formed in the water and the back of a huge animal rolled up to the surface. We pulled in our oars and dove for the floor. I said a quick prayer, expecting that we were going to be swallowed by a whale. Jack was hunkered down beside me, but

when he heard a watery snort coming from the animals in the water, he recognized the sound.

"Manatees," he whispered.

We peeked over the side of the boat. There were three animals in the water, each one as big as our boat. They looked like enormous gray footballs.

"Manatees," Jack said again. "Real live manatees! Get up, Sandy. They won't hurt us."

We crawled back up on the seat and watched the manatees in the moonlight. One at a time they lifted their heads, and when they did, we could hear them breathing.

"They're mammals," Jungle Jack explained. "They need to breathe air."

Jack held on to the side of the boat and rested his chin on his hands. He was in wildlife heaven.

"Jeesh! Real live manatees, up close, at night, in the wild."

We watched the manatees move slowly in the water for as long as they stayed near the boat. When they finally swam away, we started rowing again.

We saw other things in the moonlight as well. Big fish were chasing after smaller fish. We saw their wakes and heard their splashes. Jack spotted a round pink thing bobbing on the surface. At first we thought it was some bald-headed guy floating facedown in the water. We rowed closer and saw that it was only a Styrofoam buoy attached to a yellow rope. It was scarier when we thought it was a dead bald guy. I thought I saw a big shark fin slice up out of the water and then go back under. It only lasted a second or two, but it made the hair on my neck stand up. I didn't mention it to Jack.

We were in mid-stroke when the bow of the boat hit something hard, stopping us dead. It was the channel marker! I pulled out the map and held the flashlight on it.

"Look, Jack. We hit the channel marker shown on the map."

Jack walked his fingers across the chart to measure the distance from Key Largo to the marker.

"We're two miles from shore! The island can't

be far from here," he said, and just as he said it, he glanced over the back of the boat and saw the same big fin I saw earlier.

"Dolphin," Jungle Jack said matter-of-factly.

"How'd you know that?" I asked. "It looked like a shark to me."

"Sharks cut through the water in a straight line." Jack used his hand to show me. "And dolphins go up and down, up and down, like this." He made an undulating motion with the same hand. "That was a dolphin. We don't even want to think about a shark with a fin that big."

We rowed and rowed and didn't see the dolphin again. Jack and I took turns twisting around to see where we were headed. The sky and water were pitch black. There was no sign of the mangrove island. Back toward shore, Key Largo looked far away. Even the moon seemed farther away. Now it was higher in the sky and looked a lot smaller than it did when we first saw it rise. Jack twisted around again and this time he saw something.

"Sandy, look! There are mangroves in the water."

"The island," I said as my oar struck bottom. "We're close. It's really shallow here."

We rowed toward the mangroves, keeping our oars higher in the water so they wouldn't drag in the shallows. The *Libertad* floated over the humps and bumps of the sandy bottom. We could hear the muffled sounds of birds moving from branch to branch in the dark trees. I pulled harder on my oar once, then again, to turn the boat and bring us broadside to the mangroves. Jack tied us up to a big, sturdy root.

The waxy mangrove leaves shone in the moonlight. The little tree's long curved roots standing up out of the water looked like hundreds of big spooky fingers reaching down to clutch the sandy bottom. I waited for Jungle Jack to spout out more natural facts about mangroves, but he didn't say anything. He was getting sleepy.

The moon shone brightly on the water we had just rowed across. The distance and the quiet made me feel happy and free. For the first time ever, I wasn't worried about anything—not Dad's drinking, or even Mom. I didn't feel responsible for them or for Terry or for Jack. I was responsible only for me, and it felt great. It was as if my whole life happened the way it did just to get me to where I was—in a boat beside a tiny island in the freedom of the dark wild night. And nothing, not Dad stomping in to smack me around for his own problems, or Mom going nuts in front of the TV, or the awful memory of Terry's fall, was going to make me feel bad.

We ate handfuls of dried fruit and drank some water. Then Jack crawled into the bow of the boat and lay down. I crawled in next to him and spread our new camp blanket out to cover us. We hadn't slept much for the past two days. Jack fell asleep right away. I stayed awake awhile, staring up at the shining leaves and listening to my brother snore. Then I closed my eyes, and that's all it took.

CHAPTER 5

In my sleep I heard a *crunch!* and felt the boat jerk down violently. I stirred and woke to another jerking *crunch!* The whole back half of the boat was gone! And what remained was being chomped away by an enormous crocodile! I kicked myself backward deeper into the point of the bow, poking Jack to wake him up.

The monster croc opened its refrigerator-size mouth and bit right through the center seat.

Crunch! Its bite took a huge, jagged chunk out of the wood. Then the thing began climbing up onto the deck to get *us*! I punched Jack until he woke up, and when he did, he stood, pulled off his shirt and threw it at the croc. Then he grabbed our new filet knife, clamped its blade in his teeth and dove right into the ferocious croc's open mouth!

"Braakk!" Another loud sound shocked me truly awake, out of my dream and into daylight.

"Braakk!" the bird croaked again. It was a big, white, long-legged bird perched on a branch above our boat. The egret didn't like us being there and pooped on the boat just to make sure we got the message.

Jack was already awake, teasing the bird, flapping his elbows like wings and sticking his neck out.

"Brawk. Brawk," he called to the egret.

"Braakk!" the egret answered. They both kept it up until the egret rose up off the branch and flew across the water.

The sun hadn't come up yet over the mangroves, but its soft yellow light was streaming through the tangle of stems and roots. Something moved on the root we were tied to. It was a tiny crab. The crab climbed the root and then the mangrove stem until it was way up above the water. Jack spotted more of the tree-climbing crabs. We were watching one crab together when suddenly, from behind a thick stem, a long sharp beak stabbed the crab in the center of its shell. A little blue heron stepped out from behind the tree stem, the crab stuck on its beak. We watched the heron flip the crab around, crunch it up and swallow it down.

"We could eat those crabs too," Jack said.

"Yeah, we could. But I don't think they'd have much meat in them," I pointed out.

"We could eat them shells and all," Jungle Jack said.

"You could," I said, "not me."

We made breakfast by eating handfuls of Cheerios and washing them down with gulps of water. "I wish we had some milk," Jack said.

"This isn't so bad." I reached for the dried fruit and added a crispy banana slice to my handful of Cheerios. It tasted sweet.

Jack put some raisins on his Cheerios. He gave me the thumbs-up.

A pelican flew over the mangroves and splashed down. The big bird swam back and forth, getting closer and closer to our boat.

"He sees us eating," Jack said. "I think he wants us to give him some."

"Don't give him anything!" I told Jack, remembering when Mom once gave a french fry to a seagull and before we knew what happened hundreds of gulls were flying around us.

But Jack didn't listen. He threw a piece of dried fruit to the pelican. And wouldn't you know it—the bird had friends! Pelicans came in gangs out of the mangroves, squawking and flapping and splashing around in the water, begging us for food. When we wouldn't throw them any, they flew up onto the gunwales of the boat and snapped their bucket bills at us, trying to take the pieces of fruit right out of our hands. We had to pull off our shirts and swing them at the beggars just to keep from getting nipped. The pelicans finally gave up on getting any handouts from us and flew away.

"I told you, Jack!"

"I know."

"I told you not to . . . "

"I know. I know!" Jack said. "But it was cool swatting them with our shirts! Wasn't it?!"

"Yeah, Jack. Cool," I agreed.

The water near the mangroves was very shallow but full of life. A small stingray moseyed by, and fast-swimming schools of tiny green minnows flashed. Jack spotted a fat little fish with blue stripes on its sides and looked it up in our fish book. It was a grunt. Whole gangs of grunts were hanging around our boat. And there were other, bigger fish that Jack said were snappers. His fingers were flipping through the pages of the fish book we'd bought as fast as the fish swam by us.

"Sheepshead, porkfish, parrotfish," he called out, pointing to each new species he saw. He got so excited by all the fish in the water, he dropped the book and grabbed his snorkel mask. But I reminded him that we still had a long way to row to get to Crocodile Swamp and we should be shoving off.

So we untied the boat and rowed back out into the water of the big bay. Soon we were moving right along with perfectly matched strokes, singing as we pulled on the oars.

"Yo-ho, yo-ho, yo-ho, yo-ho," we sang in our deepest pirate voices.

The sun was up and hot. Jack wrapped his T-shirt around his head. I made a hat out of one of the brown grocery bags we got from Kmart.

"We should've bought sunblock," I said to Jack.

"Maybe we'll pass another shore with a store," Jack said.

"Maybe." I was sure we wouldn't see any more stores the closer we got to Crocodile Swamp.

I spotted the rolled-up mast and sail in the boat and wondered if they would give us some shade.

"Hey, Jack—let's try to sail across the rest of the bay."

"Good idea!" he said. I guess he figured somehow that I would know how to sail. I didn't. But I was ready to try anything to get out of the sun and not have to row the remaining two miles across the bay.

"How hard could it be?" I mumbled as I unrolled the sail, which was already attached to the wooden mast. The mast fitted nicely in a hole in our seat, and it stood up all by itself. All I had to do was hold on to the loose end of the sail. As soon as I did, the sail snapped full of air, and with the wind on our backs, we were sailing across the bay!

Waves splashed gently against the bow as the *Libertad* skidded along under its small sail. A great big manta ray shot by and Jack yelled back for me to see it. Then one by one, dolphins surfaced, each one racing the other as they followed the boat. It was almost too cool to be true. We shouted each time a dolphin's shiny gray back humped up out of the water. They looked huge, almost as long as the boat, and their swimming motion made strong waves in the water that we could feel rippling through the *Libertad*'s hull. The dolphins stayed with us for a long time before they all suddenly vanished underwater.

We were halfway across the bay when we began seeing other boats. Some of them were small with one or two people in them. Others were big with lots of passengers on board. It was fun being out on the water with the boaters. We waved at every boat we passed, no matter how far away it was. And everybody that saw us waved back.

It sounds crazy, but being in a beautiful place and experiencing something wonderful can make you think about unhappy things. The warm air, tropical breeze and clear blue water made me think about the snow and leafless gray trees back home, and Mom. If she *was* hurt, I hoped somebody found her and called an ambulance. While

Jack and I were sailing our boat on sparkling waves, I wanted to believe Mom was okay, or if she wasn't, that she was at least alive.

It took us a lot longer than we thought it would to sail all the way across the bay to the narrow channel that cut through the mangroves. In the windless channel we stopped just long enough to lower the mast, roll up the sail and eat some canned sardines and dried fruit. Then we rowed. We rowed all afternoon.

It was almost sundown when we rowed under a tall highway bridge. My arms ached. Jack's hands were beginning to blister. He lay down to rest.

"I'm ready to fall asleep," he said through a yawn.

It was low tide. The rocks of the bridge pilings were half dry and half wet. In the shadow under the bridge I spotted some movement. I squinted to make out what it was.

"Those rocks are moving," I said. Jack sat up.

"Those rocks aren't moving. Those are rats!" he said.

"Rats?"

"Yeah. Rats climbing all over the rocks."

Then I saw them too. "Rats. Jeesh! Look at 'em all!"

We let the boat drift closer. Just like Jack said, the boulders were covered with rats all out of their hiding places, scavenging around in the rock crevices for garbage or dead fish, anything the tide might have washed in.

We continued to drift under the bridge. On the other side, a few old fishing boats were tied to their moorings, but there were no fishermen in sight. It was the end of the day.

"Looks like we're all alone here," I said.

"Just us and the rats," Jack agreed.

The *Libertad* drifted slowly along, leaving the bridge and the rats and the fishing boats behind. All by itself, the little boat rounded a mangrove island where, hidden by the branches and leaves, there was a big old boat. The boat had lots of windows with screens. A rusty chain held the bow of the boat fast to the mangrove roots. The low tide had the boat grounded, resting on the sandy bottom.

I picked up my oar and used it to pole our boat closer. A little brown duck swam out from behind the big boat and began circling ours, quacking loudly.

"She must be nesting in the mangroves," Jungle Jack said.

I poled the *Libertad* to a few feet away from the

old boat. Then I held the oar out of the water and let us drift. Jack stood on the seat.

"Look at this old tub!" he said. "It's covered with garbage!"

The decks were piled high with cans, box springs, hoses, buckets, broken wooden ladders and a couple of old cracked rowboats. Some cooking pots were lined up neatly along the rail.

"Somebody must've lived here," I said. "Those pots were for collecting rainwater to drink."

The door to the cabin was open. It was dark as night inside. Jack noticed a rope hanging off the boat and dangling all the way down to the water. "I bet whoever lived here had a small boat to go places in. They kept it tied to that rope."

"*Quack quack quack quack.*" The duck was circling us again. But we paid it no attention. We were busy looking at all the junk piled on the old boat, and we started calling out each new thing we saw.

"Old washing machine."

"Crab trap!"

"Broken TV."

"Fishing pole."

"Dirty sock!" We were laughing out loud.

"A boot with a hole in the toe."

"*Quack quack quack quack.*" The duck swam by the *Libertad*'s bow, making as much noise as we did.

"A pair of holey underpants!" Jack yelled out. And we howled, laughing together. "HOLY UNDERPANTS!"

"*Quack quack quack qu*"—*kersplash*! In a splash of water, the duck disappeared! We stopped laughing. The only things left of it were a few brown feathers floating in a swirl of water. Then I saw Jack pointing. He had spotted a crocodile— it had eaten the duck! We could see the animal's head and back moving away. The water *wooshed* with the slow sideways motion of the croc's long tail.

The crocodile swam past a signpost sticking up out of the water. We read the sign together:

CROCODILE SWAMP—KEEP OUT.

"We're here," Jack said in a voice that came out small. Halfheartedly, he raised his hand for a high five, but I didn't give him one.

"We're here all right," I said, "and so are they."

We were both scared. Seeing the croc made us think twice about following it. But it was getting late and we had come a long way. So Jack and I swallowed our fear, rowed away from the garbage-smothered boat, past the *Keep Out* sign and over the invisible boundary line into the swamp.

CHAPTER 6

CROCODILE SWAMP

The water in Crocodile Swamp was about five feet deep, and surprisingly clear. Even in the dimming light we could see bottom. There were deeper holes here and there, and countless mangrove islands, some big and some only four or five feet across. In the low tide, shoals of sand showed brown in the water. And where the shoals were above the tide, the sand was white. Big black flies buzzed around and landed on the mangrove roots.

There were little lizards to eat the flies, snakes to eat the lizards, birds to eat the snakes and crocodiles to eat them all. We saw a small croc eating a snake on a curved mangrove root. As we passed, the croc plopped into the water, with the snake still clamped in its mouth.

The air was as still as the water. We could hear distant splashing sounds of fish feeding or crocs feeding on fish, and the soft feathery flapping of bird wings flying into the mangroves to roost for the night.

We never did make camp. We were so tired from rowing. Not far from the highway bridge, we tied up to the first mangrove island we bumped into.

Night blackened the mangrove islands first, then the water, and finally the sky. Out in the dark the splashing sounds became more frequent. Some were close. I took out one of the candles we had bought and lit it, letting the hot sticky wax drip on the boat seat. I stood the candle on it and turned to Jack.

To my surprise, he was crying softly.

"What's the matter, Jack?" I asked him.

"Nothing." He wouldn't face me.

"Why are you crying?"

"I'm not crying!" He sniffed. "It's just all I ever wanted, is all. To run away and live in the jungle. But not like this . . . not without Mom . . . and with Terry gone. . . . But we're here now, and . . . and . . ."

"And what, Jack?"

"And we're gonna die! We're gonna get eaten up by a croc or something! I just know it! And I'm scared!"

I put my arm around my brother's shoulder.

"Look, Jack. I need you to be Jungle Jack out here. Sure it's scary, now. It's nighttime. And we saw our first crocs. But we're safe inside the boat. *Our boat.* Tomorrow you'll feel better. I promise."

Jack wiped his eyes with his arm.

"We'll do whatever we have to, Jack. We'll catch fish for food. And anything else we need— we'll take!"

"Like pirates!" Jack said, smiling.

"That's it—pirates! You and me!" I slapped him on the back and Jack made a hook with his fingers.

"Arrrr!" he growled.

Late night in Crocodile Swamp was quiet. In the silence of the swamp, I could hear my heart beating and my lungs breathing and my brain thinking.

Jack and I huddled close to the candle. It made just enough light to brighten the boat and make us feel like we were inside rather than out in the open. Jack cozied even closer to the flame. He had the black marker pen from Kmart and began to draw a tattoo on his left arm, just above his wrist. It was a picture of a scary crocodile skull and two crossed bones.

"There, Sandy. That's us! The Pirates of Crocodile Swamp."

I leaned in to see Jack's tattoo up close.

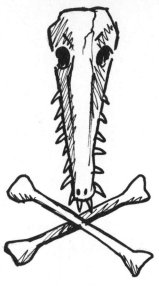

"Make me one," I said, and Jack began drawing on my arm. After he had outlined the croc skull and crossbones, he held his arm up against mine and added a little line here and there on each of our tattoos until they looked exactly alike. I took the marker and made a little line of black dots around each of my wrists and all the way up my arms. Jack grabbed the marker back and did the same to himself.

I don't know why, but the tattoo made me feel different—like I was never a kid who lived in a town or went to school or rode in a car. I felt like a real pirate who lived on the water and took what he needed and didn't need all that much.

Somewhere out in the blackness, something big splashed, but Jack and I didn't even flinch at the sound. We were caught up in the spell of the candle's flickering light. Jack suddenly picked up the fish knife, cut off a thick clump of his own hair and threw it out into the water. I touched a finger to the candle's hot dripping wax and used a glob of it to spike my own hair. I did it again and again until my whole head was spiked with tiny hardened points of wax. Then I blew the candle out.

"What'd ya go and do that for?" Jack asked.

"It was getting a little spooky around here," I answered.

"It's spookier now with no light at all," Jack protested.

"Let's go to sleep, Jack. We don't need any light to go to sleep."

I crawled up in the bow and covered myself

with our camp blanket. Jack slid in next to me.

"We had a good day," he said, and I replied, "We sure did."

While we slept, the tide came back in. I must have sensed our boat slowly rising because I dreamed about the water getting higher inch by inch. I dreamed that the rats were drowning as the barnacle-encrusted boulders under the bridge became flooded. In my dream, the fishing boats were all bobbing higher on their moorings and the old boat covered with garbage creaked and moaned as it rose up off the sandy bottom. Then suddenly, I was dreaming about Dad. He was happy and laughing and bouncing Terry on his leg. Mom was singing in the kitchen and Jack was watching sharks on TV. In my dream I knew I was dreaming. I knew it wasn't real. But I kept dreaming anyway. I didn't want to wake up. I wanted to see how long the happiness could last.

When I opened my eyes, it was morning. Next to me, Jack popped awake and looked around.

"I gotta go," he said.

"Go? Go where?"

"Go. You know. Take a dump!"

"No," I told him. "Just hold it."

"Hold it? For how long? Forever? I can't hold it! I gotta go."

Jack climbed out of the boat and onto the mangrove roots that were sticking up out of the water. Walking on the tangle of roots, he disappeared behind the thick stems and leafy branches. I called out to him.

No answer.

"Jack. You okay?"

Nothing. I waited, then yelled louder.

"*Jack!*"

"I'm here, Sandy. Stop yelling!"

Jack made his way back out. There was something green on his head. A leaf? He didn't seem to know it was there. When he climbed back in the boat, I saw that it was a small lizard.

"Guess we'll have to find a regular spot to use," he said as the lizard crawled down his forehead. "Someplace the tide washes over every day—What! What the—yikes!"

Jack smacked himself, slapping at the lizard just as it leaped off his face and onto a nearby tree stem. I was laughing so hard, now I had to go.

Making camp was fun. We tied the boat front and back to the strong mangrove roots. Mangrove trees are small—only ten feet or so above the water. But beneath the water, the trees' roots reach deep and are anchored firmly in the bottom. We set up the mast and used it to tie a line from the boat to the mangroves for hanging wet clothes. We unrolled the sail and draped it over the back of the boat to make a shelter. At the opening of this tiny tent we hung the mosquito netting, though so far neither of us had seen or felt a mosquito.

We moved our food and the water jug under

the tent where it was shady and cool. I rigged the fishing rod with a sinker, hook and plastic bobber. The rod, tackle box and bait jar were stored out in the open bow of the boat. Jack stood in the bow and admired our new home.

"Nice and simple," he said.

We ate a late breakfast of Cheerios and fruit, and then sat back in the boat to take it easy. Jack spotted something on a nearby island. He dug out the binoculars for a closer look.

"Holy underpants!" he said. "That croc must be ten feet long!"

I snatched the binoculars from Jack and refocused them on the spot. There was a gray-colored crocodile draped heavily over a small mangrove island.

"Whoah! That is a bruiser! Stay over there, big guy. Nice crocodile."

There were three other crocodiles in sight, all much farther away and smaller than the croc on the nearby island.

"Let's call that big one Annabelle," Jack said.

"How can you tell it's a girl?" I asked, half expecting him to know.

"I don't know! I don't care!" Jack said. "All I'm saying is, I saw something on TV once about an eleven-foot crocodile on an island somewhere, and the people on the island all called the croc Annabelle."

"This one's almost eleven feet long," I said, looking through the binoculars again. "Maybe it's the same croc. Maybe it swam here!" I joked.

Just then Jack grabbed the back of my leg with his two strong little hands.

"Grrrrraugh!" he growled.

I screamed and dropped the binoculars overboard into the swamp.

"What's with you?! Are you *nuts*?" I yelled. "Look what you made me do!"

We looked down into the water and saw our binoculars resting on the sandy bottom. A big blue crab scooted by the lenses. Across the water, Annabelle dropped her lower jaw and held her mouth wide open.

"That's how they rest the powerful muscles in their jaws," Jack said.

We stared at Annabelle's gaping mouth with our own jaws dropped in awe. The mouth was pink inside and full of long, sharp white teeth. She could easily swallow me or Jack! I felt the hair on my neck tingling. This couldn't be good, I thought. I looked down into the water at our drowned binoculars, and again at the huge crocodile across the way.

"Oh, well," I said, "we don't really need binoculars. Do we, Jack?"

"Yes, we do!" Jack had stripped down to his underpants and was pulling on his snorkel mask. "I'm going in to get 'em."

"Jack! You can't go in the water."

"Sure I can."

"There are crocodiles here!" I pointed to Annabelle. "Big enough to eat a kid!"

But Jack wouldn't listen. He seemed fearless.

"Annabelle? She's not gonna come all the way over here," Jungle Jack explained. "She's been hunting all night. She's probably stuffed with a big fat raccoon."

Jack fitted the mask to his face, blew through the breathing tube to make sure it was clear, then removed it from his mouth to add, "She'll be digesting all day long."

With that, he sat on the gunwale, put the snorkel tube back in his mouth, held his mask with the palms of his hands just like divers do on TV, and let himself fall backward into the water. He swam down to the bottom and came back up with the binoculars in one hand and the big blue crab in the other. I found my paper bag hat and let him drop the crab into it. I wondered how he caught that crab with his bare hands. Then he dove again. I could see him down there approaching another crab. He swam close to the crab and reached for it. The crab raised its claws. Jack tried for it again. This time the crab pinched his hand and drew blood. I could see red oozing from the wound and swirling away in the water.

Jack tried for the crab again, using his left hand

to get the crab's attention and his right hand to grab it from behind. It worked! Jack swam up holding the claw-clicking crab high. It went in the paper bag hat with the other.

"Come on in, Sandy!" Jack said. "It's fun!"

I looked at Annabelle over on her island. She wasn't even facing us now. Her mouth was closed. Her eyes looked closed. It was just like Jungle Jack said. She wasn't going anywhere. I stripped down, pulled on my snorkel mask and climbed down into the water to join my brother.

Underwater, everything looked different—more spectacular than it looks from above. The sunlight made a fan of yellow rays that you could swim through like a liquid curtain. Fish looked bigger and you could see each one's eyes and mouth and fins. There were hundreds of minnows shining emerald green as they surrounded Jack and me. Also swimming with us were grunts and snappers. The snappers looked huge. One snapper could make a meal. Jack approached a particularly large snapper and tried to grab it with his hands, but the fish scooted away.

We could keep our faces down the entire time, as long as we kept the ends of our snorkels sticking up out of the water. I lifted my head to adjust my mask and Jack popped up beside me.

"Let's see what it looks like under the mangroves," he gurgled, and we each took a deep breath and dove under together to look.

With our lungs filled with air, we swam beneath the *Libertad*, where a colorful parrotfish was nibbling at the growth encrusted on the boat's bottom, and we continued on to the mangroves the boat was tied to. Underwater, each long mangrove root was covered with long strands of orange algae. And beneath the algae, small snappers were hiding, all stacked up like things on a shelf. We swam down the edge of the roots and found snappers behind every one. We stayed under for as long as we could hold our breath. Then we rose together in the water and swam back to the *Libertad*.

I climbed up first and was helping Jack when I spotted a huge gray fin cutting through the water, heading right for us. My chest tightened and my heart pounded against my ribs.

"Shark!" I yelled.

Jack turned to look and saw the fin coming toward him.

"Yaaaahhhh!" he yelled, scrambling to get up into the boat.

I grabbed Jack by the armpits and pulled him up with one great heave. *Swoosh! Thump!* The shark

rushed by us, bumping the canvas hard as it passed. Jack grabbed his oar and held it high, ready to whack the shark if it tried to come back and eat the boat. I grabbed my oar to do the same.

The shark swam around us in a slow arc. From nose to tail tip, it was at least ten feet long.

"Hammerhead," Jungle Jack said. "Look at that monster! Coulda bit me in half! Thanks, Sandy."

The shark was making another slow pass when it quickly turned and rushed us again. I swung down with my oar, hitting the water with a loud *smack!*

"Don't do that!" Jack said. "Those kinds of noises or motions in the water attract sharks."

"What attracted it to us?" I wondered out loud. "We weren't making any loud splashes. We were just swimming quietly."

Jack held up his hand and showed me where the crab pinched him. It was a deep cut and still oozing a little blood. He squeezed it with his fingers and a gush of fresh blood welled up from the wound, dripping down onto the gunwale of the boat.

"Sharks can smell blood," Jack said, squeezing more out of the cut. "All it takes is a drop to attract a shark."

"Stop that!" I panicked. "Don't bleed in the boat! Your blood could soak in and we'll never get it out. Sharks will come from all over to eat our boat!"

I was half crazy with the idea of sharks coming to get us. I grabbed Jack's hand and shoved it in his mouth.

"Suck that! Suck it until it stops bleeding!" I said.

"Yeth thur!" Jack said sarcastically, sucking his hand.

The hammerhead made another pass.

"That thing's just pacing back and forth like a tiger in a cage, waiting for supper," Jack said, never taking his eyes off the shark.

"Yeah, and we're supper!" I yelled, as Jack watched the shark.

The shark passed again, closer. Its big dorsal fin sliced through the water just the way you see in movies. Only this was no movie. It was real. Too real.

"It's the same color as Dad's Chevy," I said.

"It's a killer," Jack said, following the shark with his eyes. "It swims and kills. That's all it does."

CHAPTER 7
BIG FISH

*T*he hammerhead was the biggest fish Jack and I had ever seen outside of an aquarium or a zoo. It cruised around our boat for another hour or so, until the tide turned and the water became so shallow it could no longer swim near us. Jack stepped out of the boat onto the curved mangrove roots. Then he walked from root to root to a tiny lump of land that wasn't there earlier. A small tidal beach was forming near the mangroves.

"It's okay to walk on," Jack said, and I walked over the roots to where he was. The sand of the little beach wasn't really sand. It was broken bits of what looked like crushed coral.

We walked around looking at everything closely. Jack found a tiny conch shell. I found a blue crab leg. Where the high tide had flooded the mangrove roots, they were covered with tiny snails that looked like coffee beans. Jack was getting hungry again, and he wondered if the snails were edible. He pulled one off a root and put it in his mouth.

"Gross!" I said, while Jack gagged and spat the shell out.

The more the tide went out, the bigger our beach became. Soon we were wandering all over the place, touching and marveling at everything we saw. We chased lizards and snuck up on birds. We collected shells and fish bones and chunks of coral and buried it all in a secret spot like real pirates buried their treasures.

Jack set up our tiny stove on the beach and heated our frying pan full of salt water to cook the crabs he had caught earlier. When the water was boiling, I plopped in the crabs. After a few minutes, their blue shells turned bright red, and we had fresh crabmeat for lunch. Being cooked in salt water made the meat extra salty, but we didn't mind. It tasted good to us.

When the tide was at its lowest, I rigged the fishing rod with some dead minnows from the jar we had bought, cast it out as far as I could, and propped the rod on a beach boulder.

Immediately, my bobber dunked under. I grabbed the rod and yanked a ten-inch snapper out of the water.

"Fish for dinner tonight!" I howled. Then one right after another, I caught three more.

Jack checked our fish book to see if snappers were good to eat. They were. And there were even instructions on how to clean them for cooking. He spread the book and held it open to the instructions with a small coral boulder. Then, going by the pictures in the book, he stuck the sharp point of our new fish knife into the first snapper's belly and slit it open. Jack reached inside the fish with his fingers and pulled out the guts.

"Ugh!" he said. "Sandy, hold my nose. This stinks!"

I held Jack's nose and my own. Jack chopped off the fish's head and peeled off its scaly skin. What was left was like the fish you would buy at the grocery store.

Jack didn't need me to hold his nose while he cleaned the remaining fish. He was getting used to the smell and it didn't seem to bother him anymore. While he worked, I got the stove going again, and in no time at all we were eating fried snapper, smothered with sweet dried fruits. It was the best meal I'd ever eaten and I had to lick my fingers before washing them in the water. Jack scooped up all the fish guts and bones and

skin from the beach, and threw them in the
water. The strong fishy smell and splashing sounds
of the fish leavings hitting the water must have
reached Annabelle and gotten her attention. She
lifted her heavy head, crawled over the mangrove
roots and slid into the water. Jack and I grabbed
all our gear and ran to the boat.

"You'd better throw that stuff a little farther
out next time!" I said to Jack as we ducked down

inside the *Libertad* and watched Annabelle approaching.

The croc swam slowly to where Jack had tossed the cleanings. Then she sank, just like a great big water-soaked log. Air bubbled up to the surface. She stayed under a long time. Finally, she popped back up with a piece of snapper skin stuck to one of her long teeth. She was awfully close to us in the boat. When she chomped up the fish skin, her jaws made loud popping sounds that made Jack and me cringe lower. She must have seen us there, but she wasn't interested in us. She just wanted those fish scraps.

After she had eaten all there was, Annabelle swam away, but not back to her island. She swam out into the deeper water of the swamp, probably to hunt for more food. Other crocs were moving too. Jack counted ten, most of them far away.

Our bellies were full. We felt good. Jack and I went back to the beach and cleared a place where we could lie without getting poked by sharp coral. We weren't afraid of the crocs out in the water.

We could live with the crocs as long as they didn't get too close.

The hammerhead did scare us. I hoped it wouldn't return with the tide. But right now, on the warm beach, surrounded by crocodiles and snakes and who knew what else, I felt perfectly safe. It was like having our own tropical island a thousand miles from civilization. It was hard to believe that just five miles away there was a town with people and stores and traffic.

The next day high tide came in the middle of the afternoon and with it, a feeding frenzy of big fish. Annabelle slid off her island and swam away.

"She's after the big fish that are eating all the little fish," Jungle Jack said.

I rigged the fishing line with the largest hook in the tackle box and baited it with three minnows from the dead minnow jar.

"Make sure you cover the whole hook with bait," Jungle Jack said, and that's what I did.

There wasn't a bit of metal hook showing when I cast the line from the boat.

As soon as the bait hit the water, a huge fish swirled up and grabbed it.

"Whooooa! Jack! I got something! It's big!"

Jack hopped up on the seat to get a better view. My line was cutting through the water, and at its end a huge silver-sided fish was yanking and tugging, struggling to get loose.

"Let some line out, or he'll break free," Jack coached.

"How? He's pulling too hard."

"Turn that drag thing the guy told you about."

The fish was running now and my rod was bent nearly in two. I glanced at the reel and remembered the drag knob on top of the spool. I held on to the rod with my right hand and used my left hand to turn the knob. *Wham!* The line tightened up so fast my rod jerked downward, and hit the side of the boat.

"Turn it the other way!" Jack yelled, and as soon as I did, the rod straightened up and the line started peeling off the reel as the fish ran with the bait. I could feel its power through the line up my arms, and into my back.

This was nothing like catching snappers. This was something else. I was happy and excited. I felt strong and brave and weak and scared all at the same time. It was new and strange, but somehow I felt like I had been doing it all my life. Fighting that fish felt as natural as running or jumping or swimming underwater and coming up for air. I bent my toes up and pressed them against the wall of the boat and just held on as the fish pulled off half the line I had on the reel before suddenly slowing down. Then the line went slack.

"I lost him!"

"No, Sandy, he's turning around! Look at the line moving in the water. Reel in the slack! Reel! Reel!"

Jack was jumping up and down on his perch. I reeled like crazy, cranking in line until I felt the weight of the fish again. I could see it out in the water now, shining silver just under the surface.

The big fin on its back and its wide tail were both waving up out of the water. The fish had to be at least as long as me.

"Awesome!" Jack said, as he started leafing through the fish book. Just then, the fish leaped high out of the water and flashed brightly in the sun.

"*Tarpon!*" Jungle Jack screamed.

"Holy underpants!" I shouted, seeing what I was up against.

"Good thing the boat's tied to these roots!" Jack said.

The tarpon splashed down and ran again. I tightened my grip on the rod handle and leaned back against Jack's legs.

"He's heading for those mangroves!" Jack squealed. "He'll tangle up in the roots! Tighten the drag! That'll slow him down."

But the huge fish didn't slow down. It kept powering away toward the distant patch of mangroves. The strength of the tarpon's pull was more than I could handle. I fell forward, banging my elbows on the boat, but I didn't let go. I held on to the rod with both hands and jammed its cork butt into my belly. Then I yanked with all my might. Jack grabbed me around the waist, squeezing my gut so tight that I could hardly breathe.

"Yank on him again!"

I put every muscle in my body into one last yank. It worked. The tarpon stopped just short of the mangrove roots and flipped over on the surface. I reeled in as much line as I could while the fish thrashed. Then I heard Jack say something but couldn't make it out. I was too busy trying to get my finger back on the drag to loosen it a little. The fish was really jerking me around.

"Hammerhead!" Jack shouted in my ear.

I shot a look where he was pointing and saw the shark's fin break the surface.

"Reel! Reel as fast as you can!" Jack screamed.

The tarpon must have smelled or felt the shark coming and panicked. It started swimming in circles with its green back humping up out of the water. When the fish felt the pull of my line again, it dove momentarily and then shot up out of the water, making a high somersault before belly flopping down. The hammerhead zeroed in on the commotion. I reeled so hard and fast, the butt of the rod against my stomach ripped a hole in my T-shirt. I yanked and yanked, pumping the fish closer, pulling the heavy, worn-out tarpon through the water. The shark swam faster, until it was within striking distance of my fish.

"Reel! Reel! Reel!" That's all Jack kept saying.

"I am!" I said. "I'm reeling as fast as I can!"

Then, in an instant, my line went slack, and the tarpon disappeared in an explosion of bloody water. In the center of it all, the hammerhead rolled. Its big gray fin waved out of the red pool, and then sliced under as the shark carried the tarpon away. I reeled in my line and all that was attached to it was the tarpon's head. Jack and I looked at it for a while hanging down in the water. Then Jack cut my line and the head drifted away. My mouth was so dry, it hurt to swallow. I went to get a drink of water and found only a few cupfuls left in the jug.

"We're almost out of water," I told Jack.

Jack swished the water around in the bottom of the jug.

"We'll have to get more," he said. "Back at the bridge. That garbage boat. I bet there's water in those pots lined up along the rail."

"We'll go tonight," I said. "After we eat something."

"You mean canned sardines. That's all we got left."

"Yep. That's about it."

"Yuck."

My shoulders ached and my hands were sore. The muscles in my arms felt tight and hard. While Jack opened a can of sardines, I just sat in the boat thinking about the fish I had lost.

*T*he tide was still high at sundown. After our sardine supper, we undid our tent and rolled up the sail. Then we untied the *Libertad* and shoved off. Annabelle was back in the water near her island, and we kept an eye on her as we rowed.

"That crazy croc's starting to follow us!" Jack said, and he was right. Annabelle seemed to be swimming along in our water trail. We pulled harder on our oars to leave her behind, but she swam faster, her long white teeth showing in the rippled wake around her mouth. Her big tail was swooshing back and forth, propelling her along.

"She's gaining on us!" Jack said as he pulled on his oar. I rowed in time with him to keep the *Libertad* heading straight. As I hauled back on my oar, I spotted something else trailing us, halfway between our stern and Annabelle's snout. It was a length of loose rope we had forgotten to coil and stow, dragging in the water. It looked like a water snake slithering on the surface.

"She thinks that rope's a snake!" I told Jack. "That's what she's after. Not us."

Annabelle raised her huge head out of the water and chomped on the rope with her massive jaws, pulling the entire length into the water. The wet rope flipped over in the water and draped across Annabelle's eyes. She raised her head again and chomped until the whole rope was down her enormous gullet. Then she lowered her jaws back in the water and swam away.

"That's just dessert," I said to Jack, laughing as we rowed.

"Yeah, a little rope to go with all the fish she probably ate today," Jack said.

"I thought she was after us!" I said. "That was spooky having her follow the boat like that."

"Did you see how she lifted her head up to chomp that rope?" Jack asked.

"Yeah, I was right here. Remember?" I said.

"No. I mean, it reminded me of something . . . her lifting her head like that with her front teeth showing. Remember that guy Dad brought home with him once from Tony's Bar? Henry? Was that his name?"

I knew the guy. Dad was always bringing his goofy drinking buddies home for Mom to meet. This guy Henry wasn't goofy. He was weird. He ate glass.

"He ate glass," Jack remembered just as I was thinking it. "He sat at our kitchen table and ate a whole lightbulb! Remember? He held his head up as he chomped the glass, just the way Annabelle did eating our rope."

"Yeah! And he had pointy teeth too!" I said.

"Remember how it sounded? All that sharp glass crunching in his mouth."

"Shut up! You're giving me a stomachache!" I told Jack.

I rowed along with Jack, thinking about that Henry guy. I knew Jack was too, because every so often he'd shiver his shoulders, trying to shake the image of it out of his mind.

There were more crocs in the water. A few were six-footers, one was eight, easily. But none of them came close to Annabelle's size. We rowed right by them like we were on a safari park ride. A flock of long-legged pink birds were wading in a cove. Jungle Jack said they were spoonbills. The birds walked in the shallow water, heads down, using their long, spoon-shaped bills to stir up the bottom and catch any food hiding in the mud. The spoonbills' rosy-colored feathers were beautiful in the orange light. Three brown pelicans flapped down over our heads. They were heading for their mangrove roosts for the night. A lone egret squawked as it landed on a high branch. And everywhere, fish were jumping, making bright silver circles on the dark water.

I thought about Henry again. He was the same guy who brought us the horse. Dad must have found out Henry had a horse and asked him to bring it by so we could ride it. I don't know where Henry lived, but he walked that horse the whole way. He didn't ride it. It was a big golden palomino. That's what Henry said, and he called it Chub. Terry was just a baby. I was eight. Jack was six. Henry lifted me up onto the saddle. The leather made little twisting noises when you moved on it. Jack sat in front of me and I held him tight as Henry walked Chub down the driveway and onto the road. Once in a while Chub threw his head back and whinnied. When he did, his yellow mane swished over our hands.

We rode that horse all the way down our road and back. Dad was waiting for us in the driveway. He had the biggest grin on his face. It was a rare happy memory of Dad and I was about to see if Jack remembered it too when he said, "Hey, Sandy, look up!"

We were gliding under an overhanging branch and on the branch was the shadowy form of a coiled snake. As we passed beneath, I could see that the snake was solid orange in color.

"What kind of snake is that?" I asked.

"I don't know. But it isn't poisonous."

"How can you be so sure?"

"Because there are only four kinds of poisonous snakes in North America. Rattlesnakes, copperheads, cottonmouths and coral snakes. And that isn't any of them—that's how."

I was impressed. I wondered just how much of that kind of information my little brother had jammed in his brain. He always amazed me with the things he knew about animals. He amazed me in lots of ways. He was stronger than me.

When we wrestled, he always came out on top. He was braver than me. And he was harder on Dad than I could ever be. I was about to ask him again if he remembered our ride on Chub when he said slyly, "I bet I know what *you're* thinking!"

"What?" I asked.

"You're thinking about the garbage boat and that old rotten pair of underpants!"

"Holy underpants!" we said together, and our voices echoed across the water.

"What do you think Dad's doing right now?" I asked Jack.

"He's probably getting drunk in some Key Largo bar. What else would he be doing?"

Jack was right. And the image of Dad sulking in some bar, cursing us and the whole world, made me forget all about Henry and riding Chub and Dad grinning at us in the driveway.

The sky was deep blue and the moon had risen by the time we rowed by the boundary sign and out of the swamp. We rowed as quietly as our squeaky oars would let us, rounding the mangrove island where the garbage boat was tied. We were surprised to see a light on inside the cabin.

"Somebody's in there!" I whispered.

But the fact that the boat was occupied didn't deter Jack. "We need to get closer, so I can climb up to the pots," he said.

I raised my oar and held it up out of the water. Jack did the same. We drifted noiselessly closer to the trash-covered tub, until I could reach up and hold its rail while my brother hauled himself on board to get to the water-filled pots. Jack moved silently along the edge of the high boat. He wasn't alone. Every time he took a step or reached to hold on to the rail, something rustled in the piled-up trash. Suddenly Jack stopped.

"Rat!" he whispered.

Of course! With all that garbage, there had to

be rats. The whole pile was probably infested. My mouth got dry with fear for Jack. When he finally made it to the first pot of water, I moved near and held our jug high for him to pour. Then he put the empty pot back down and picked up the next. I held the jug up for that water too.

Jack was going for the third pot of water when I spotted something moving just inches away from his hand, and I yelled, "Snake!"

I jumped up on the big boat and pushed Jack away just as the snake struck. It missed, falling clumsily off the edge of the boat and plopping into the water. Jack was a mess! He was lying on a pile of trash and his feet were all tangled up in a wad of fishing line. He kicked himself free, but before we could jump down into the *Libertad*, somebody grabbed us both from behind. We struggled and kicked. Jack swung his arm around trying to punch the guy, but whoever he was, he was strong and held us just out of arm's reach.

"What have we here?" he said, like he was

talking to all the rats and snakes on his filthy boat. He pushed our faces toward the garbage until we were eyeball to eyeball with a big coiled snake. And he held us there as the hissing snake slowly backed deeper into the pile.

"Let us go!" I yelled.

"Let you go? Oh, no. I can't let you go. Not until I find out what you were doing. What did you steal from me?"

"Nothing," Jack growled. "Just let us go!"

"Nothing? I see my water pots have been emptied. Would you steal an old man's water?"

He led us over the junk pile, through the open cabin door and down some steps into the belly of the big, smelly old boat.

The man sat Jack and me down—both of us kicking and swinging—on a black bench in the corner of his cabin. Only one small lightbulb lit the room and it was getting power from two long wires attached to a car battery on the floor. The floor and walls, and even the ceiling, were all paneled in dark wood. Hanging from the ceiling were what seemed to be hundreds of shark jaws, in various stages of drying out. Some had bits of flesh and blood stuck to them. All of them had rows of sharp white teeth.

The walls were covered with carvings of fish and other animals. A long white elephant tusk stood in one corner. It had the figure of a mermaid scratched into it. Next to the tusk a native mask covered the wall from floor to ceiling. The mask showed a face of someone screaming.

I was really scared. I opened my mouth to yell for help but, like the face in the mask, nothing was coming out.

The man picked up a knife from the kitchen table and walked over to us. He put a small stool right in front of the cabin door and squatted, staring at us the whole time, and running his big thumb back and forth along the knife's sharp blade. One of Jack's legs started to tremble. I put my hand on his knee to help him calm down.

The man was really old. His hair was pure

white. He had wrinkles all over his face and a short white beard that grew up his cheeks almost to his eyes and down his neck to his hairy chest. He was tall and muscular. His eyes were small and dark. He wore sneakers with no socks, jeans and a brown undershirt. There was a leather cord around his neck with a big white shark tooth hanging on it. When he sat up, the tooth rested against his chest. When he leaned forward, the tooth dangled in the air. Both of his arms were covered with old tattoos that were green and blurry-looking. There were daggers and skulls and barbed wire and bleeding roses and words I couldn't make out. Only one tattoo was clear and colorful. It was a picture of the Blessed Mother surrounded by rosary beads.

A green iguana, about a foot and a half in length, darted out from under some junk and ran to the man. The lizard climbed the stool and up the man's back until it was on top of the old guy's head, where it stayed facing us.

"Do you see, Little One?" the old man said, looking up to the lizard. "We have caught a couple of bandits. What should we do with these thieves?" He spoke with a Spanish accent.

Jack's leg started going again.

"This place stinks!" he shouted. "And you smell too!"

"You don't like my smell?" the man asked. "I say you boys smell a little ripe yourselves. I may have to soak you both in brine before I make a stew out of you."

I figured the guy was joking, but Jack didn't. His back stiffened and both of his legs began to jump and quiver.

He was looking all around the room for a way to get out or for something to whack the old guy with, when he spotted a hammer lying on the floor and ran and grabbed it. He looked like he was going to explode.

"You aren't gonna make stew outta anybody!" Jack said, holding the handle of the hammer with both hands.

"Drop it!" the old man demanded as he leaned forward on his stool, pointing his knife at Jack.

"Stay back!" Jack yelled. "Don't you move! You ain't gonna cook us or beat on us. Nobody's gonna hit us. Never again! From now on, I'm gonna do the hittin'!"

Suddenly the old man's glare softened. He lowered his knife and eased off.

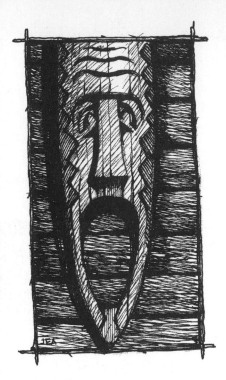

*T*he old man put his knife down on the floor and lowered the iguana down with it.

"Put the hammer down, boy," the man said, "before somebody gets hurt."

"Somebody *is* gonna get hurt," Jack answered. "You!"

The old man looked at me, then turned back to Jack.

"Take it easy, son. I'm not going to hurt you. I

was just trying to frighten you, so you'd leave me alone. I can't afford to have two boys hiding in the swamp and stealing from me every time they run out of water."

"How'd you know we were hiding in the swamp?" I asked.

"Why else would you be stealing my water?"

"What were you gonna do with that knife?" Jack asked, lowering the hammer.

"I was going to cut some baloney and fry it up. Would you like some fried baloney?"

"We already ate," Jack said, but my stomach was growling. We'd only had some sardines and I said we'd eat.

"Bueno!" the old man said. "Come. Sit at the table."

We went to the table and slid onto the booth seat. The iguana climbed up the table leg, over the tabletop, and up a pole to a shelf above us. It was bright green and blue with black spots. Its long tail was yellow with black bars.

"What kind of lizard is that?" I asked the man.

"It's a green iguana," Jungle Jack said. "They're native to Central and South America."

"You know your lizards!" the man said. "Little One is a pet someone abandoned. He found my boat and we've been friends ever since. Right, Little One?" The iguana dipped its chin as if to agree.

"We're sorry for trying to steal your water," Jack said.

The old man sat at the table with us and poured three glasses of water. He used the knife to slice a lime in half and squeezed the juice into our drinks. Then he picked up his glass, touched it to his chest and introduced himself.

"Alfredo."

"Sandy."

"Jack."

"Are you a pirate?" Jack asked.

"No." Alfredo laughed. "I'm just an old fisherman." He spotted the crocodile skull on Jack's arm. "You are the one who looks like a pirate!"

"We are pirates!" Jack said. "We're the Pirates

of Crocodile Swamp!" He pulled my arm close to his and we showed Alfredo our matching tattoos.

"*Bueno!* Very nice," Alfredo said. "Tell me, what brings you boys to Crocodile Swamp and a life of piracy?"

We told Alfredo our story from the time Terry died to our escape in the freedom boat. I did most

of the talking. Jack added details. It was the first time either of us had spoken to a grown-up about our home life. Alfredo's forgiving us for trying to steal his water made us trust him. He let us talk and when we finally stopped talking, he asked, "And your mother—you are sure she is dead?"

"We think so," I said.

"I'm sure!" Jack said. "Like we said, Dad killed her!"

Alfredo made the sign of the cross on himself just the way Mom used to do. Something squeaked outside on the deck.

"Rat. Gone," Alfredo said, making his hand into a snake shape and snapping at us with it.

"Why do you let rats and snakes live on your boat?" I asked. "Why don't you chase 'em off or kill 'em?"

"The rats eat the garbage, and the snakes eat the rats," Alfredo answered. "Besides, they're out there, and we're in here." He looked up at the iguana. "Right, Little One?"

The lizard dipped its chin.

"What kinds of snakes do you have?" Jungle Jack asked.

Alfredo thought for a second or two, then he said, "Mostly there are water snakes. They are not venomous. The snake I introduced you boys to earlier—that was a water snake. Then there are cottonmouths. They are venomous. There are cottonmouths living in the small freshwater pools in the woodlands around the swamp. I'm afraid a few have discovered my boat and made it their home."

"Why do you call them cottonmouths?" I asked Alfredo, but Jungle Jack answered.

"They have a white lining on the inside of their mouths that looks like cotton."

"That's what we saw on the deck near the water pot!" I told Alfredo. "That's what tried to bite Jack!"

"The snakes do like to coil near the water pots to cool off," Alfredo said, turning to Jack. "You are lucky, my young knowledgeable friend. You must know that if that snake would have bitten you, we would all be in Tavernier right now, in the Mariners Hospital, and you would be a very sick boy. Oh yes, cottonmouths can be deadly."

Jack completely missed the gravity of what Alfredo said. He was charged up about the kinds of snakes that were living on Alfredo's boat.

"What else?" Jack asked.

"What do you mean?" Alfredo replied.

"What other kinds of snakes do you have?"

I just shook my head and squeezed more lime into my water.

"Oh—the snakes. Occasionally I see a rattler. We have big diamondbacks here. You boys be careful of them in the swamp, especially on the few dry islands. That's where the rattlers live. Occasionally you will see them in the water swimming from one dry island to another."

He got up and went over to the stove, where he lit a burner with a long wooden match and set a big black frying pan on the flames. Big slices of onions were already in the pan.

"And, of course, there are the lovely little orange mangrove snakes."

"We saw one!" I said. "It was up on a branch. We rowed our boat right under it!"

"Count yourselves lucky. They are rarely seen. I can remember seeing only four or five in all the years I've been here."

Alfredo opened the fridge and took out a big length of baloney. Jack and I had never seen it in one big piece like that. We saw them in the meat counters at the grocery store. But in our house we only knew sliced baloney.

Alfredo peeled back the outer covering and began slicing, dropping the pieces into the hot pan. They sizzled as they cooked and soon the cabin smelled like suppertime.

Alfredo went to the fridge again and got a whole carton of eggs. One by one, he cracked the eggs open over the pan, letting their yellow yolks fall onto the baloney. When he had cracked open half the eggs in the carton, he took a spatula from a wall hook and used it to shovel the whole mess together. The fried meat spat and spattered in its own grease. The hot eggs snapped and popped as they cooked. The smell made my mouth water. Jack's stomach growled loudly.

There was another squeal topside, and Jack and I looked at each other and said together, "Rat. Gone."

"That will do it!" our cook said, turning the mountain of food over with the spatula. Then he shut off the burner and began scooping baloney and eggs and onions out of the pan and onto three plates. He carried the plates to the table, set each one down with a fork beside it and sat with us to eat. But before we did, he lowered his head to pray thanks for the food. Jack and I lowered our heads and said the dinner prayer Mom taught us.

"Lord, thank you for this food which we are about to receive from Thy bounty. And thank you for the company of those with whom we share this meal."

Alfredo waited for us to finish and ended his

prayer with us, "In the name of the Father, Son and Holy Ghost. Amen."

I watched Alfredo as he ate. He didn't seem as old anymore—just worn, like a pair of shoes or faded jeans. His hands and fingers were huge; his fingernails were cracked and ragged on the edges. His skin was deeply browned from a lifetime in the sun, even inside the wrinkles of his face. And every hair on his head and face and chest and arms was as white as the big shark tooth he was wearing.

"What kind of shark tooth is that?" Jack asked, with an onion ring hanging out of his mouth.

Alfredo held the tooth out from his chest and looked down at it. "This is a tooth of a great white," he said. "That shark was twenty feet long! I killed it along with at least fifty other smaller sharks in one day—lemons, tigers, bulls and black tips."

Then Alfredo got up and took some lettuce from the fridge to bring to the lizard. "I know, Little One. You are hungry too."

The shelf above the table was crowded with photos. One of them was a photo of a man standing next to a huge shark. Alfredo took down the photo for us to see up close.

"That's me during the war, with one of the sharks we caught by throwing dynamite into a lagoon. The blast dazed the fish and they floated up to the surface. The small ones we ate. Small sharks are good eating, remember that in the swamp. Any big one we caught we took to port to trade for supplies or souvenirs. Some sharks we skinned ourselves just for the jaws. People buy the jaws. I still sell some to shops in the Keys."

Jack and I stared at the photo trying to see Alfredo in the younger man pictured. Jack touched the photo with his fingers and measured the hanging shark. It was at least two feet longer than the man.

"Whenever we happened to stun a large shark, we'd hang it up and take a picture. Hanging it by the tail like that also made sure it was dead. Hanging a shark upside down suffocates it. That was the way we did things back then. It was an easy way to catch fish of all kinds. For years I would stun fish, but not with dynamite. I used firecrackers like these."

He took three small red balls down from the shelf and handed them to Jack.

"I never saw firecrackers like these," Jack said.

"Those are little Fourth of July cherry bombs. They are old. Pretty powerful. They don't make them anymore. I don't use them on fish anymore either. They have to go off at precisely the right moment, before they hit the water and fizzle out. I use them now to frighten away cormorants whenever too many of them perch on the boat. Rats and snakes I can live with. A ton of bird guano, that is something else."

Alfredo got busy clearing away the dishes and glasses and slices of lime on the table. I saw Jack slip one of the cherry bombs into his pocket and put the others back on the shelf.

When Alfredo finished up the dishes, he sat at the table again.

"That boat you boys have. That is the one the Cuban family came over on last year, is it not? I've seen it on the shore at Petruzzo's place."

"That's the one," I said.

"You won't tell anyone we have it, will you?" Jack asked.

"Absolutely not!" Alfredo snapped. "When you live on the water you learn to keep what you see and hear to yourself." He thought for a moment. Then he said, "Those refugees sailed through a terrible storm. I remember when they arrived. Everybody was talking about it."

"Refugees?" Jack asked, puzzled by the word.

"Refugees," Alfredo repeated, placing both arms on the table. "People who flee persecution or war, or because they want freedom they cannot have at home. You boys having to run and hide in Crocodile Swamp—*you* are refugees."

He reached over, smiling, and rubbed Jack's head. "You are brave boys. My people sailing from their homeland in such small homemade crafts; they are also brave."

I figured Alfredo was Cuban because he called the refugees his people. I wondered if he came over in a homemade boat himself, but before I could ask, he changed the subject.

"How are you set for supplies?"

Jack and I told him what stuff we had bought for our camp. As he listened to each item he sometimes nodded in approval, and sometimes shook his head no.

He went to a small desk in a corner of the cabin and picked up a paper and pencil. Then he came back, sat on the same side of the table as us and began to make a list of things he thought we should have.

He stopped writing and asked, "Do you boys have any money?"

I told him we did, and he didn't ask how much or where we got it.

"*Bueno!*" he said. "And I'll give you more, so you can pick up a few things for me."

"Where are we going?" Jack asked.

"Shopping," Alfredo told him. "You can take

my skiff to the Petruzzos' beach. Its little out-board engine will get you there and back in less than two hours."

"But that's where we stole our boat from," I reminded Alfredo.

"So?" he said. "No one saw you—did they?"

"No."

"Then nobody knows what happened to that boat. Besides, you'll be in *my* boat. That should clear any suspicions people may have about you."

Jack slapped Alfredo on the back. "You really *are* a pirate!" he said.

The clock on the cabin wall chimed twelve times. It was midnight, but none of us felt tired. We talked about fish, snakes, sharks and living on the water. The more Alfredo talked, the more I liked and admired him. I decided not to ask him too much about his past. It seemed too much like prying. He was here now and he had made him-self our friend. That's all that mattered to me, but not to Jack.

"Where did you come from?" Jack asked.

"I was born in Cuba," Alfredo said. "I spent my young life on that island. We were poor. We all had to pitch in. As a boy I fished every day with a hand line to help provide food for my family. Later, during World War Two, I worked on a salvage boat hauling wrecks off the reefs."

"Did you like living in Cuba?" Jack asked.

"It was my home."

"Why'd you leave?" Jack and I asked together.

"Well. . . ." Alfredo paused, looking thoughtful for a moment. "After the war, our country got all caught up in change. A revolution, we called it. But I didn't like the changes it brought, so I left."

"On a homemade boat?" I wondered out loud.

"No. No. The homemade boats came much later," Alfredo said. "I had a job working on a freighter and when we pulled into Miami one day, I just stayed."

Alfredo reached up to a shelf and clicked on a small radio. It was tuned to a Spanish music station. The music was soft and slow and it made us all feel sleepy. Alfredo dozed off in his chair. I folded my arms on the table and put my head down. Jack did the same.

The next thing I knew, Alfredo was waking us up, pointing to daylight coming through the cabin window.

"*Buenos días!* Good day!" he said.

"*Buenos días!*" we said, only half awake.

After giving us each a glass of orange juice to perk us up, Alfredo motioned for us to follow him. We went out onto the deck and walked over the trash to the rail. Little One only came with us as far as the door, stopping at the threshold.

"He's afraid of rats," Alfredo said.

I was watching out for snakes and rats the whole way, but there weren't any, at least not out in the open.

"There she is!" Alfredo pointed down to his

skiff. "You boys know how to run an outboard, don't you? The gas is on. Just pull the starter rope. Steer with the tiller arm, left to turn right, right to turn left. Go slow until you get into the channel. By then you'll have gotten the feel of it."

He pointed down the channel in the direction of town. "Follow this the way you came. Petruzzo's is only eight miles away. You can beach the boat there and go across the highway for supplies, just as you did before."

Alfredo threw an empty five-gallon plastic jug down into the skiff.

"Fill this with water for me. Frank and Marie don't mind boaters filling up at their dock. Don't forget to bring your own jug along."

Jack climbed down a ladder that was nailed right to the old boat. I followed him and we sat in Alfredo's aluminum skiff. Alfredo looked down at us. Then he looked at the *Libertad*.

"I'll watch your boat. Don't worry."

Jack was in the center seat. I was back near the engine. I pulled the starter rope, but the engine only chugged and did not start.

"Choke it a little," Alfredo called down from the deck. "That knob on the back? It says Choke. Pull it out and pull the starter rope again."

Jack came back and found the knob before I could. Then I pulled the starter rope again. *Whirrr!* The little engine started creating a cloud of blue smoke.

"Now push the choke knob back in!" Alfredo yelled. And when I did, the engine stopped smoking and purred like a cat.

"Forward," Alfredo instructed, twisting his hand as if he was turning something in the air. I found a lever on the side of the engine that had three settings marked F, N and R. I pushed the lever to F and popped the engine into gear. Jack untied the line and, going very slowly, I steered the skiff toward the *Libertad* so we could grab our empty water jug. Alfredo was waving from the high deck with more instructions.

"Give it more gas by twisting the tiller grip. The tide is out. Watch the water color. If it is green or blue, sail on through. If it is brown, it's too shallow and you will run aground," he called as we motored away. I steered the skiff, pushing the tiller right to turn left away from the mangrove island. We passed the boulders under the bridge, and went into the channel. The sun was already hot on our heads.

"We may have been refugees when we started," Jack said to me from the bow of the skiff, "but we're pirates now! Go fast, Sandy!"

I twisted the tiller grip, giving more gas until we were roaring along as fast as the little engine could push us. I felt as free as the birds flying high over the mangroves.

"Awesome!" Jack shouted as we raced down the channel toward town.

We powered for Petruzzo's beach, keeping
to green water all the way. When we were close,
I steered the skiff toward the sandy shore
and slowed down. The tide was extra low,
the bay visibly shrinking away from the shore.
I spotted Mia walking around on the restaurant deck. She was busy putting fresh flowers
on each of the waterfront tables. We had
almost reached the beach when the propeller

hit bottom and the engine conked out. Jack and I hopped out and pulled the boat the rest of the way.

"Next time we'll tilt the engine up when we come in," he said, pointing to a few small boats nosed onto the beach. They all had their outboard engines tilted forward with their props up out of the water. I tilted our engine like the others. It was easy. I just pulled it toward me and the engine pivoted forward, raising the prop a foot or so into the air. Jack waded back and inspected the propeller blades. Hitting bottom sounded worse than it was. The prop was fine.

Together Jack and I muscled the boat up onto the beach and wedged its bow into dry sand. Gulls swooped and dived, snatching tiny crabs that the receding tide had left high and dry. We were concentrating so much on the boat and the gulls, neither of us noticed that Mia had come down to the beach and was standing there, watching us. She was wearing shorts and a T-shirt. And she looked angry.

"What did you do with my father's boat?" she asked point-blank.

"What boat?" Jack replied, trying not to look Mia in the face.

"You know what boat!" she said, angered further by Jack's obvious lie. "The *Libertad*. The freedom boat! You stole it!"

"This isn't your father's boat!" Jack said.

"I know it isn't!" Mia was livid. "This is Mr. Sanchez's boat! He beaches it here whenever he comes to town. Did you steal it too?"

"Who's Mr. Sanchez?" I asked.

"You know who he is! You've been at his place in my father's boat. I know it. The local fishermen know it. One of our customers saw you there this morning. He told Daddy and he told your father too. He was just here, having a cup of coffee."

That was a bomb we didn't expect. Jack stepped up to Mia as if he was going to punch her and I pulled him back. But he shook me off, and marched up to Mia.

"How do you know about our father? You gotta tell us!" Jack demanded.

"Yeah, Mia," I said. "It's important. We stole your boat. I admit it. But you said a freedom boat doesn't belong to anyone except those it carries to freedom."

"And we were wanting freedom," Jack said.

Mia softened. She walked back to the deck steps and sat down. "Freedom?" she asked. "From what? From who?"

"From our father!" Jack said. "And you gotta tell us what you know about him."

"Please, Mia. We need to know. Jack and me, we're scared for our lives!"

Mia told us what had happened just an hour earlier in the restaurant. A local fisherman named Carlos told her father he had seen the *Libertad* tied up to Alfredo's boat. He saw it as he was driving over the bridge, and he said he saw two boys in Alfredo's skiff.

"There was a stranger sitting at the end of the

counter holding his head," Mia said. "Daddy figured he had a hangover and gave him a free cup of coffee. Hangover coffee's free in our restaurant. The stranger heard Carlos mention two boys, and asked what they looked like. When Carlos described the two of you, the stranger wanted to know where Alfredo lived. Daddy and Carlos told him how to get there and that he'd need a boat because the bridge crosses over swampland, and there's no way to get from the highway to Alfredo's on foot. He stormed out without a word. Not even a thank-you for the coffee."

"How'd you know it was our father?" Jack asked.

"I'm just guessing it was," Mia told Jack. "He had the same sandy-colored hair as your brother." She turned to me. "And he combed it straight forward the way you do, or did, before your new look." Now she was laughing. I had forgotten all about the wax, which was still sticking to my hair! It must have really looked weird.

"You say he thinks we're living at Alfredo's?" Jack asked.

"Aren't you?"

"No," Jack bragged, "we're living in Crocodile Swamp."

"Crocodile Swamp?" Mia was horrified. "It's too dangerous for you in there! Nobody goes in there! It's strictly off-limits to the public!"

"We know," Jack said. "That's why we went. Dad will never look for us in there. He'll never think we'd be living with all those crocs."

"I guess!" Mia said. "But why would you live with crocodiles instead of being with your father? Where's your mother?"

I took a chance that Mia wouldn't tell on us and told her our story just the way I told Alfredo. Only this time, when I mentioned the part about what we were afraid Dad did to Mom, Jack started crying. "He killed her and he'll kill us too if he finds us!"

"Yeah, Mia," I said. "We can't tell anybody the

way things are. We're afraid we'll get put in some home."

"They'll bust us apart," Jack cried.

"Don't you see?" I said. "We gotta hide where nobody will find us. Please don't tell anybody what we told you. Crocodile Swamp is the only place for us now."

Mia looked at me. "I'll keep your secret. But you've got to promise me you'll be very careful in that place. And you have to stay away from Mr. Sanchez's. Your father will be looking for you there."

"We promise," I said.

"What if your father goes to the police himself and reports you two missing?" Mia asked. "The whole island will be out searching for you then."

"He won't go to the cops," Jack told her. "He doesn't want to be found either."

"No, I guess he wouldn't," Mia said.

"Yeah." I added, "Don't worry, Mia. We can take care of ourselves. But we gotta go back to

Alfredo's. We're here to pick up supplies for us and some things for him. And we gotta bring back his skiff."

By the time we had finished shopping and filling the water jugs, the tide had bottomed out. We had to drag the skiff over ten feet of wet sand to get to where we could shove off. And once we did, the skiff, weighted down with two heavy water jugs, sat deeper in the water. Jack used an oar to pole us out to where it was deep enough to lower the prop and start the outboard.

I steered us slowly back out into the bay, watching the water color like Alfredo said—"green or blue, sail on through." Whenever we came to a patch of water that looked brown, we went around it. And if it was too big to go around, I tilted the outboard up a little so we could go over the spot without hitting bottom. Jack helped by climbing forward and sitting up on the point of the bow. He was just heavy enough to raise the back of the boat and the prop an inch or two more.

Neither of us said much all the way down the mangrove channel. As we were going under the bridge, I asked Jack if he thought Dad would be waiting for us at Alfredo's.

"He doesn't have a boat," Jack said. "Not yet. And by the time he gets a boat, we'll be back in the swamp."

Tying up to Alfredo's wasn't easy. A wind had suddenly picked up and was blowing straight down the long channel. The waves bobbed the skiff up and down. Jack had to hold the rail of Alfredo's boat with both hands to keep the skiff from banging hard against the wooden ladder. I stumbled and fell trying to tie the front and back of the skiff to the big boat. When I finally got the knots right, Jack climbed up the ladder, dragging Alfredo's water jug. I climbed up behind him, pushing the jug from below to help him haul it over the rail and onto the deck. Then I went back down to the skiff for the groceries. The sun was high but there were no snakes out on the deck. Jack quietly pushed open the cabin door and we went inside.

Alfredo was on his small bunk sleeping flat on his back with the iguana on top of him. The lizard looked like it was sleeping too, eyes closed, its chin facing Alfredo's bearded chin. The iguana's green scaly head was resting on the old man's hairy chest.

We were about to leave when Alfredo woke and sat up, the iguana sliding and falling to the floor, where it quickly came to its senses and crawled under the bed.

Alfredo looked at the table and the bag of groceries we had brought him.

"*Gracias,*" he said. "And did you fill the water jugs?"

"Yep!" Jack answered.

"The skiff . . . she ran good?"

"She sure did," I told him.

"*Bueno! Bueno!*" Alfredo said happily. But when he stood up, he let out a howl.

"Ayeeee! Old bones. You're wearing out!"

He plopped back down on his bed. Then, using one of the long wooden masks from the wall as a crutch, he stood again, slowly and very painfully.

"What's wrong with your leg?" Jack asked.

"Not my leg. It is my hip. It fails me at times. Sometimes I can barely get on my feet. I will be fine. I am old. That is all. Too old, I think."

"How old are you?" Jack asked Alfredo.

"Seventy," Alfredo answered.

"Seventy? Years? That's almost a hundred!" Jack shouted.

"Not quite," Alfredo said, "but sometimes I feel like it. And when I think back over the years— all the things I have seen and done—it seems like more than a hundred."

Alfredo crutched himself painfully across the room to his desk and brought back two rawhide necklaces, one for me and one for Jack. Each had a bright white shark tooth hanging on the leather.

"I made them when you were in town. I made them in honor of your great adventure," Alfredo said, draping a necklace over Jack's head to rest around his neck. Then he put mine on me.

We thanked him as he sat down slowly and folded his hands on top of the table. We told him what Mia had told us—that Dad might come around looking for us. Alfredo listened, then sat saying nothing for almost a whole minute. Finally he spoke.

"Boys. I want you to think hard about your father. Is there any way you can approach him and talk to him . . . and ask him what he did, and what really happened to your mother?"

"No way!" Jack said.

"I don't think so," I said. "I wish we could. I wish we could stop being afraid of him and that he'd stop being afraid of us telling on him, and . . ."

"I don't wish nothing!" Jack said, pounding his fist on the table. "I want him gone! I want him dead!"

Alfredo held Jack's fist to the table. "Listen to me, Jack. You can't let yourself feel that way. Yes, you want him away from you. You want him to leave. You want him to be who he is away from you, so you can be who you are without him. But you don't want him dead."

Jack started up again, but Alfredo held Jack's fist more firmly on the table.

"Someday your father will be dead. Everyone dies. But if you don't make some peace with him while he is alive, the memory of him will always be lurking, making your life about him and not about you. I know this. I had a difficult father. He was a man I thought I hated, just like you think you hate your father. But what I learned when I left Cuba and finally got away from my father's house was that I had such strong feelings for him because I loved him. Not because I hated him."

"But how can you love a person who makes you want to hate him?" I asked.

"You try to understand who that person is apart from you. That is the only way you can know who you are apart from him."

"Huh?" Jack was confused. So was I.

Alfredo opened his hands on the table top and used them to make the shape of a bowl.

"Think of your father as a vessel that is filled with everything he ever heard and saw and felt. Everyone he has ever known. Every place he has ever been. Every pain. Every hurt. Every little triumph. Every happy moment. Every dream he ever dreamed. Every mistake. Every failure. All of these things are what makes your father who he is, and makes him different than you boys. Think of him this way and it will be easier to forgive him. You don't have to go back and live with him. But you must eventually forgive him or he will be stalking your lives forever . . . even after he dies."

"But what about the things you are born with? Like how we have the same color hair and the same shaped noses. Things like that. Don't they make us the same?" I asked.

"Those things are what you are, not *who* you are. How you live; the things you learn; the way you use your talents and skills; your experiences; these are the things that determine who you are."

"I don't get it!" Jack said, pulling his hand out from under Alfredo's. "I'm okay hatin' Dad! I'd like to fill a big bowl with hate and crack the thing on his skull!"

"That is entirely up to you, my young friend," Alfredo said, dropping the subject.

"You don't know our father," Jack continued. "He's a killer, just like that hammerhead we got swimming around in the swamp."

"He'll be looking for us. You better watch out," I warned Alfredo, "he will hurt you. He punches and pushes people. He might push you down on your sore hip."

Alfredo hobbled over to the cabin door and stepped out. "There is no one around here now. You boys better go. Take my skiff to tow your boat back into the swamp. Make your camp and use my boat to get around."

"Awesome!" Jack said.

"Bring it back in a couple of days. I won't be much good in a boat for at least a few days. Then you can bring me my skiff and row back in your own boat."

Alfredo stepped and a pain shot up his side.

"Aieeee!" he cried out. "Three. Maybe three days. I'll be better then. Now go!"

We helped Alfredo walk slowly inside and back to his bunk. Then we left and climbed down into the skiff. As I tied a tow line to the *Libertad*, I thought about Dad and what Alfredo had said about forgiving.

CHAPTER *11*
HANGING A HAMMERHEAD

We motored slowly and quietly back into the swamp with the *Libertad* following on its tow rope.

"Jack. . . ." I paused, afraid to say what I was going to say. "I'd like to try to talk to Dad, like Alfredo said."

"I don't want to talk to Dad about anything!"

"But, Jack—"

"Forget Dad! I don't wanna talk about him no more!" Jack said emphatically.

We cruised along on the returning tide. The wind had died down, and the water in the swamp was calm. A few crocs were swimming. Seeing crocodiles actually made me feel safer. They were the reason no one would come here, I thought. No one except Jack and me. And I stopped worrying about Dad. Jack also had something else on his mind. He reached in his pocket and pulled out the cherry bomb.

"That's Alfredo's!" I said. "I saw you take it. Why?"

"I'm gonna get rid of that hammerhead," he told me, holding the small red bomb by its fuse right in front of my nose.

"You figuring on chasing it away with that little thing?"

"No, I'm gonna *kill* it with this little thing. We're gonna kill it!"

Jack sat up tall in his seat so we were eye to eye.

"We're gonna knock it out with this, and then

hang it up. Just like Alfredo said. Remember? Hanging a shark upside down suffocates it. That means it *kills* it! That's how we're gonna do it."

I slowed the skiff down to a crawl, took the cherry bomb and held it. It was heavier than I thought it would be.

"You really think this can knock out a ten-foot shark?"

"Yep."

"But Jack, you're the one who's always repeating stuff you hear on TV... how sharks are being hunted down and they might become endangered."

Jack grabbed the little bomb back.

"This shark's already endangered, because I'm gonna kill it!"

Jack was all wrongheaded about the hammerhead. I knew it and he knew it. Jack knew more about sharks than any other animal. He loved sharks! That hammerhead wasn't after us, but Jack let himself believe it was. He couldn't do anything about Dad chasing us, but he could do something about the shark. He was wrong, but I played along with him anyway.

"So what if we do kill the shark?" I asked. "What'll we do with it?"

"We'll bring it to Alfredo for the jaws and the teeth," Jack said.

I touched the shiny shark tooth on my new necklace. The thought of us adding another big-toothed shark jaw to Alfredo's collection appealed to me.

Jack dangled the cherry bomb in front of my face again.

"Shark. Gone!" He grinned, and that made me laugh.

"Shark. Gone!" I said, imitating Jack's grin. "You win. We'll do it! We'll hang that overgrown sucker and give him to Alfredo."

We were going to get our chance. The hammerhead was a creature of habit and we were camped where it hunted for food. With the tide on the rise it would most definitely be back.

As we pulled into our cove, we got a startling welcome. Annabelle suddenly swam out from behind a mangrove clump, bumping her huge side against the skiff as she passed. I freaked and almost crashed the boat into the trees. But she wasn't after us. She was after something else and we had gotten in her way. When the massive crocodile reached the middle of the cove, she sank like a rock and stayed under. Jack pulled the tow rope to bring the *Libertad* closer, and grabbed the binoculars.

"What's she doing down under?" I wondered.

"A snake!" Jack said, peering through the binoculars. "There's a great big snake swimming out there! Have a look."

I didn't bother to take the binoculars. I just turned the skiff and putted closer until we could both see the snake better. It was a large rattle-snake; one of the big diamondbacks Alfredo said lived in the swamp. We could clearly see the dark diamond-shaped blotches down the length of its body and the rattle at the end of its thick tail. The rattler had to have been five inches thick at its middle. Its head was the size of my fist. It was swimming slowly in a sideways motion just the way snakes move on land. Suddenly, Annabelle attacked it from beneath.

"Holy underpants!" Jack yelled.

I killed the engine and the skiff sat dead in the

water while we watched Annabelle chomp onto the snake's middle with her powerful jaws. The rattler whipped its head around once and struck the thick hide on the croc's head, but that didn't stop Annabelle from chomping down again, biting the squirming snake in two. Then she raised her huge chin, flipped the lifeless rattler into her mouth and swallowed the whole bloody mess. It was gruesome! It was horrible!

"Cool!" Jack said, eyes glued to Annabelle as she swam away. He turned to me all excited. "Hurry, Sandy! Let's make camp and get ready for the shark!"

We made camp with the rising tide lapping against the two boats. Jack worked feverishly, coiling all the spare rope we had in the *Libertad* and tying the ends together. Then he tied all that to a long length of rope that was in Alfredo's skiff.

"Help me pile all this rope together," he said.

"Why? You're doing a good job all by yourself," I teased.

"Sandy, I mean it! I need you to feed me the rope so I can coil it in the bow of the skiff, all neat. Then it won't tangle up once I lasso the hammerhead."

"Lasso it?" I asked incredulously. But Jack ignored me.

I climbed into the skiff and helped Jack get all the rope just where he wanted it. A couple of big fish splashed nearby, spraying water up into the air. Then a second later at least a hundred small silver fish shot out of the water in their own kind of shower. A fish shower. The whole school of fish wriggled through the air just like they were swimming. Then they all splashed down together back into the water. They were being chased by bigger fish. The swamp was boiling with fish chasing fish.

We noticed every splash and dash in the water. Some of the chasing was being done by hungry crocs. None of the crocs was very big. Annabelle was still out in the swamp somewhere. Jungle Jack said she must have had a bad night out hunting.

"How do you know that?" I asked my brother.

"'Cause if she had a full belly she'd be on her island, lying there like a ton of rubber, digesting what she ate. . . . Yep! She must've come up empty last night. Or she wouldn't be out now, still hunting."

"What about the snake?" I asked. "She just ate that snake."

Jack climbed over the coiled rope, tied one end to the back of the boat and made a lasso with the other end.

"That rattlesnake didn't fill her up," he said. "One rattler'd be just a taste. That would just make her want more. Like one potato chip. Here, Sandy, check this lasso. You think it'll hold the shark?"

I checked the lasso's slip knot and gave Jack the okay sign, all the while marveling at what my little brother had stuffed in his head. He knew how animals lived, and what they needed to survive each day.

"Ready!" Jack said. Then he suddenly remembered something and jumped from the skiff into the *Libertad* to grab the box of matches and the fish knife.

Back in the skiff, Jack pulled the cherry bomb out of his pocket and handed it to me along with the matches. I didn't know what to expect next. Were we going to go hunt the hammerhead down? Or were we going to wait for the shark to come to us?

We waited. Jack watched the water. I watched Jack. The sun's glare on the water reflected on his face. He was squinting, looking far across the swamp.

"There he is!" Jack shouted.

Sure enough, out in the water some distance away was that huge triangle of fin ripping through the surface as the hammerhead chased a school of fish one way, then turned to chase them in a different direction. The shark had fish as big as three and four feet long rocketing up through the surface trying to escape.

"How we gonna get him to come to us?" I

asked Jack. "He's got too much to eat out there."

Jack jumped in the *Libertad* again and opened a can of sardines. One by one, he tossed the oily fish out into the water, yelling, "Here, sharky sharky! Here, sharky!"

The wind and current spread the sardine oil out from our boat and toward the shark, but the hammerhead just kept feeding on the closer, living fish. Instead of coming toward us, he was going away, chasing the terrified school farther and farther from our rope and cherry bomb plans. Jack hopped back into the skiff with me.

"Let's go get 'im!" Jack said. He untied the rope holding us to the mangroves.

I started the engine and putted slowly out toward the shark.

"Are we crazy?" I asked as I steered toward the monster in the water. Jack didn't hear me. He was busy pulling his shoes and socks off.

When we were about a hundred feet away from the hammerhead, Jack said, "Stop!" I put the engine in neutral and let it idle as we drifted closer to the feeding shark.

"What're we going to do once we lasso it?" I asked.

"We're gonna drag it with the skiff and hang it on that tree." Jack pointed to a long branch reaching out over the water.

The shark suddenly surfaced, head and back out of the water as it lunged after a leaping fish. Jack hung his legs over the side, kicking and splashing his bare feet in the water.

"Come here, you dummy!" he called out in all the commotion.

But the shark skidded after a pair of surfacing barracuda. The skiff drifted closer. We were only about fifty feet away when Jack did something that I couldn't believe. He unsheathed our sharp fish knife and sliced his own thumb, drawing blood.

"Jack!" I screamed.

My crazy brother held his hand out over the water and squeezed his sliced thumb. Huge drops of red blood began dripping from the cut and dropping into the green water.

"He'll smell it," Jack said. "He'll smell it and come."

Either the hammerhead did smell Jack's drifting blood, or it didn't, but it came anyway, swimming steadily in our direction. I grabbed the matches. Jack held the cherry bomb and the lasso. The shark swam closer.

"Wait . . . wait . . . " Jack directed. "Let him come right by the boat."

My hands began to shake and I had to press the match against the matchbox striker just to keep from dropping things. Jack raised the cherry bomb up to my match. The shark rushed toward us. I could feel its forward wake pushing the skiff.

"Now!" yelled Jack.

I struck the match and lit the little bomb's short fuse and Jack threw it right at the shark's big flat head. But it didn't go off! The fuse blew out or got wet or the cherry bomb was too old or it was a dud. Whatever—it just bounced, smoking, off the shark's skin and into the water.

The hammerhead turned quickly toward the tiny smoking ball and splashed violently on the surface, hitting the skiff hard. Jack dropped the rope and the two of us fell backward into the boat. I landed on the idling engine, accidentally popping it into reverse, and the boat took off. I grabbed the tiller and twisted the grip to get us going forward, but I had forgotten to shift the engine into forward gear. We sped backward through the water. I panicked and gave it more gas.

We were going full throttle in reverse, heading straight for a small mangrove island. Before I could gather my wits, we had reached the mangroves. Just before we hit the trees, Jack looked up and screamed.

"Snakes! Duck, Sandy, duck!"

Nestled on a high branch, hanging right over the narrow water gap between the two islands, a whole bunch of snakes were all tangled together in a ball. When the skiff rammed into the mangrove roots, all the snakes got knocked off their branch, plopping down onto Jack and me! We pulled snakes off our heads and shoulders. We kicked snakes off our legs. We screamed and yelled and grabbed snakes until every last one was thrown out of the boat and into the water.

Then Jack started to cry. And so did I. But when we realized we hadn't been bitten, we began to laugh. We rolled around in the skiff laughing, kicking our feet against the boat's aluminum sides.

Suddenly there was another sound, not ours. It was the sound of a motorboat coming fast.

CHAPTER 12
REUNION

*T*hrough an opening in the mangroves, we spotted a larger skiff with a big powerful outboard engine roaring straight for us. The man driving the boat was Dad!

"It's Dad! It's him!" Jack cried. "He sees us!"

"He must've heard us screaming!" I said.

The boat was close enough for Jack to read PARADISE ISLE BOAT RENTALS on the bow. Our engine had conked out when we hit the mangrove. I had to pull and pull the starter rope to get it going again. As soon as it did, I put it in forward and raced away.

"Lose him!" Jack yelled.

I rounded a clump of tiny mangrove sprouts, aimed the bow of the skiff at a long strip of bigger mangroves with a half hidden opening to water on the other side and zoomed through. The little engine's prop whacked bottom but kept on going.

Dad's boat followed, just clearing the mangroves on either side of the cut and hitting its prop hard on the rocky bottom. We could hear it bang from where we were, even over the noise of our engine.

We tore across open water. Jack was scared, but more angry.

"Go away!" he shouted at Dad.

"Sit down!" I yelled. Jack sat down, but kept yelling.

"I hope he hits a croc and crashes!"

Jack leaped to his feet again, shaking his fist at

Dad in the boat close behind us. "Leave us alone!" he screamed.

Up ahead I spotted a color change in the water. It was turning from green to tan. I gave the throttle a final twist and forced the little engine to go faster. "If it's brown, you'll run aground," I said to myself. Dad's rented boat was bigger and heavier than our skiff. And its engine was bigger, so its prop reached deeper into the water than ours. I could hear Dad revving it up to catch us on open water. "*He doesn't know about the brown*," I thought, and kept speeding straight for the tan patch of water.

"Jack! Climb up front and sit on the bow. We need to raise the back of the boat."

Jack saw the brown water up ahead and caught on right away. He perched on the bow and watched Dad gaining on us. Just as the water changed from green to brown, I pulled our engine forward, lifting its prop higher in the water. We skimmed right over a broad sandbar, and when we reached green water on the other side, I lowered the prop and we roared away.

Dad hit the brown patch full speed and grounded with a loud *screee* as the bigger engine's propeller plowed into sand and bottom muck until it stopped dead.

"If it's brown, you'll run aground!" Jack yelled back at Dad stranded on the sandbar.

"Shut up, Jack!" I said. My hands were shaking and my stomach felt like it was twisted in knots. I took a long route around the mangroves to get back to the *Libertad*, trying to make Dad think by the sound of our engine that we were going farther and farther away. In truth, his boat was stranded very close to our camp. But he was going to have to do a lot of pushing and pulling to get off that sandbar.

I drove the skiff up to our little island and tied it to a mangrove root next to the *Libertad*. Then we both hunkered down in the freedom boat, each of us holding an oar to use as a weapon. And we waited.

Annabelle was gone, still hunting for something

to eat. I thought I saw her in the water near some low-hanging mangrove branches, and checked it out with the binocs. But it was only a great big manatee feeding on the green, succulent mangrove leaves, its purplish-gray head the size of a basketball. The manatee moved in slow motion, rising up out of the water to nibble only tender new leaves. In the silence of the swamp and the way sound travels so clearly over water, I could hear it munching whole mouthfuls of leaves and twigs. It chewed slowly, not in the hurried way of predators or prey. The manatee was neither. It had nothing to run from and it pursued nothing. It was peaceful. I would have traded places in a second. The manatee moved away from the mangroves, rolled underwater—gently flipping its tail on the surface—and was gone as suddenly as it had appeared.

I remembered Jack and felt guilty I hadn't pointed the manatee out to him. A huge flock of white birds flew over, and Jungle Jack said they were ibises. The birds flew away in the direction of Dad's grounded boat, and I wondered if Dad would look up and see them and think they were as beautiful as I did. What kinds of things *did* Dad think about?

"I'm gonna try to talk to him," I whispered to Jack.

"Who? Dad?" Jack asked.

"Yeah, Dad," I said. "Maybe if we just talk to him and ask him to—"

"You nuts?" Jack asked. "If we get anywhere near him, he's gonna clobber us. Besides, we can't just let him off. He killed Mom and Terry. He deserves to die!"

"We don't know if he killed Mom. And Terry . . . that was really an accident," I said.

"An accident? Sandy, your head's getting soft. All that stuff Alfredo said is making you mushy. Maybe Mom's alive. But Dad doesn't care. Maybe Terry's fall was an accident, but *he* pushed Terry. Don't forget that! If he comes near me, he's gonna have an accident of his own. He's gonna run right into this here oar and get his brains knocked out!"

Jack was boiling again. I decided to keep my thoughts to myself so as not to make him any angrier. We had to keep our cool.

The sun was going down. The mangrove islands made long shadows across the water. I looked for movements on the water but the surface was as still as glass.

A ripple of unseen energy traveling through the water gently rocked the boats. Then I heard an engine whining in the distance.

"He's off the sandbar!" Jack said, and I felt my fingers tighten around the oar I was holding.

We could hear every move Dad made as he motored back and forth and circled the mangrove islands, hunting us down.

"I bet he's crazy mad!" Jack whispered as his eyes followed the sound of the rental boat's engine.

"I don't care what you say, Jack, but before

I try to kill him with this oar, I'm gonna talk to him! I'll yell if I have to. But I'm gonna say something to him as soon as he gets close enough to hear."

"Do what you want, Sandy. But if he gets that close, I'm gonna jump outta this boat and crack his head open."

The noise of the engine got a little stronger and louder each time Dad weaved back and forth through the maze of mangroves. Then the engine sound stopped abruptly. Dad had shut it off. I stood up and made my ears bigger by cupping my hands behind them so I could hear better.

"He's close. I know he's close," Jack whispered.

"Shhh!" I said. "I hear something!"

Jack stood up next to me, cupping his hands behind his ears, and we both heard the slosh of oars being rowed. But we didn't see any waves in the water or movements behind the dark mangroves. The rowing stopped, and when I heard the soft bumping sounds of oars being carefully put down on boat seats, I called out, "Dad! It's Sandy! Me and Jack don't want any trouble. We won't tell on you about Terry or Mom or anything. We just want you to leave us alone."

Jack punched me hard in the side.

"Dad?" I called out again, but he didn't answer.

"That's great! He moved while you were talking! Now we don't know where he is!" Jack said. "You and your talking! It's no good!"

Jack lifted his oar and held it like a spear. I had my oar in one hand and a coil of rope in the other.

Tiny waves of water rippled around the edge of our island and we heard the sound of legs pushing against water. Dad was out of his boat and wading. *Braak!* A white egret rose off its hidden perch and flapped away as Dad came splashing out in the open and rushed our boat.

"I've got you now! I've got you both!" he growled. "I'm gonna break your necks!"

Jack jabbed at him with the oar. I lashed at him

with the rope, but he kept coming, sloshing waist-deep in the water until he had both hands on the *Libertad*. I kicked and stepped on his fingers but he wouldn't let go.

Dad lifted himself up on the side of the boat and grabbed me by the shirt. That's when Jack swung hard with his oar and hit Dad across the back, knocking him into the water with a loud splash. Dad climbed back up on the side of the boat and went for Jack. He was madder than I had ever seen him. I pushed him and he fell back into the water, making another splash.

Suddenly, I spotted Annabelle! I guess she was swimming slowly toward her island when Dad's loud splash made her speed up and veer in our direction. I dropped my rope. Annabelle submerged.

"Dad! Croc! Get up! Get in the boat!" I screamed.

Jack threw down his oar and reached over the side of the boat to help. Dad grabbed hold of the boat, and was trying to pull himself back up, when the huge croc emerged in the water behind him.

"Hurry, Dad!" Jack yelled.

Dad turned around and saw the croc. "God Almighty!" he cried out.

Jack and I pulled on Dad together, trying to help him out of the water and up into the boat, but his heavy, wet body kept slipping back in. Annabelle swam to within five feet of Dad's legs and stopped with her mouth slightly opened and jaws raised just enough for her long white teeth to show above the water surface. Dad heaved himself up; he got one leg on the gunwale when the croc lunged, seizing the other leg in her jaws and pulling Dad, screaming in horror, underwater.

"Dad!" Jack shrieked. He dove in to help. I jumped in right behind him. We swam down to Dad, grabbed his arms and pulled as hard as we could, but Annabelle was too strong and she yanked him deeper. We surfaced for air and dove again, grabbing Dad by the armpits and tugging, only this time Jack kept kicking the monster

croc's huge head and eyes until she finally gave up and let go.

We swam Dad up to the surface and pulled him out onto the mangroves as quickly as we could, knowing Annabelle might try for him again. He was half drowned and bleeding badly. I pulled my belt off and tightened it around Dad's leg to try and slow the bleeding, but it kept pouring out of him. He sputtered and gurgled to consciousness.

"That thing really got me. It got me good!"

"Just lay still, Dad," I said as I tightened the belt around his leg.

"It's no use, son. I'm . . ." He was fading fast.

We dragged Dad higher on the mangrove roots to keep him away from the bloody water that we were still afraid would provoke another attack. The wound bled and bled and there was nothing we could do to stop it. Dad looked down at the river of blood that was emptying the life out of him. His face was pale but oddly peaceful. All his meanness and anger appeared to be draining out too.

"Bad blood," Dad said. "It ruined my father. It ruined me. Don't let it ruin you boys too." He closed his eyes.

Jack cut the *Libertad*'s sail off the mast and we wrapped it around Dad's leg so no more blood would ooze out into the water. We were still afraid Annabelle would come back. Dad opened his eyes and looked at me for a long time. I kissed him on the cheek, feeling the stubble of his beard prick my lips.

"Thanks, Sandy," he said softly. Then he looked at Jack and said, "I messed up . . . with you . . . with your mom."

"What happened to Mom?" Jack asked. "Is she dead?"

"I think so. I hit her hard. I didn't mean to hit her so hard. . . . But I couldn't stand it anymore— her sitting there moaning and talking to herself. I punched her. She fell and hit her head against the radiator."

"You just left her there?" Jack asked.

"I thought she was dead. I thought I killed her,

like I did Terry. I didn't know what to do . . . I . . ."

"Don't talk, Dad," I told him. "You're using yourself up."

Dad rolled his head back to look at the sky. I watched the sky's reflection in his eyes. Jack held Dad's hand. None of us spoke for a long while.

"Did you boys see all the white birds?" Dad asked, looking up at the fading light. "I wonder what kind they were."

"Ibises," Jack said, but Dad was already dead.

I gently closed Dad's eyes with my fingers. We stayed there with him on the mangrove roots until the sky got dark and for some time after. We had spent our whole lives hoping, planning and wishing we would get away from him. Now all we wanted was to have him back.

We held him tight and cried for him. We cried for Mom and for Terry. We cried for each other. We cried until tears no longer came and all that was left was the ache.

CHAPTER 13

RIVER IN THE SEA

*I*t took some doing, but by morning we had gotten Dad's body off the mangroves and into the *Libertad* without banging him around too much. With the center seat removed, he fit perfectly in the *Libertad,* with his shoulders in the stern and his feet toward the bow. I nestled his head against the float cushions. Then we covered him completely with the big part of the sail that wasn't wrapped around his leg, tucking him in tightly until he looked like a patchwork mummy. There was no more blood. The tide was out and most of Dad's blood had gone out with it.

Blood had soaked into the sailcloth around his leg. It was dry. But we worried about the odor of it and whether it would attract sharks to the boat. Jack found a whole bunch of oily-smelling rags under the stern seat in Alfredo's skiff. We packed them all around Dad. That seemed to do it for us. Jack and I both felt Dad's body was safe inside the boat.

I tied a rope from the bow of the *Libertad* to the back of the skiff, started the outboard engine and headed out. The *Libertad* towed nice and easy with the load. The water was calm and, with the tide going out, the current was with us. It was so early, the sun hadn't yet cleared the tops of the mangroves. Birds were still asleep in their trees. A couple of small crocs were swimming near Annabelle's island. Annabelle was gone somewhere in the swamp.

Jack hadn't said much all morning and I didn't

try to talk to him. When a pair of pelicans flew over the skiff, he pointed to them and we watched in silence as the birds flew away.

I ran the little engine at idle speed, going as slowly as possible to see everything I could on our last trip out of Crocodile Swamp. I knew we weren't coming back.

There are a lot of beautiful things to see in a mangrove swamp. Not all of them are birds or fish or other animals. A smoky fog was lifting off the water. When we cruised through a patch, Jack, sitting in the bow of the skiff, vanished for a few seconds, then reappeared. Every mangrove leaf I looked at was jeweled with dew. In places, the sun found holes in the tangle of trees and beamed through, brightening small ovals of water. In one sunlit oval I spotted minnows swimming.

Tiny waves off our bow rippled against the mangrove roots, making the roots' reflections wiggle and dance as we went by. A low-hanging leaf dragged in the current, looking as if all by itself it was trying to slow the water's flow back to the ocean.

We no longer had to hide from Dad in the swamp, but we still had to lie low. I was hoping Alfredo would let us stay with him. I was also hoping he would help us figure out what to do about Dad.

I pulled up to Alfredo's boat and Jack tied us to the ladder. Inside the big boat's cabin we found Alfredo awake but still on his bunk.

"*Buenos días,*" he greeted us.

"Morning, Alfredo," Jack said.

"*Buenos días,*" I said.

Alfredo sat up very slowly.

"I'm afraid this is as far as I'm going to get today. No matter. You boys can make us some breakfast."

I blurted out what had happened the night before in the swamp. Jack didn't say anything.

"You say your father's body is out in the boat, right now?" Alfredo asked incredulously.

"Yeah," we answered together.

"Is it covered good?"

"We covered him all up with the sail," Jack said.

Alfredo said something in Spanish. He was thinking out loud, leaning toward the window near his bunk to look out at the *Libertad*. He tried to stand, but sat right back down, moaning loudly. His hip hurt him worse than the day before.

"Listen to me, my young friends. You cannot keep that boat around here very long. It will attract animals and worse, it will attract the authorities. And then we will have a lot of explaining to do."

"What should we do with him?" I asked.

"I don't know. Let me think," Alfredo said.

"We gotta bring him out and dump him in the ocean," Jack said, "that's the only place no one will find him."

"Dump Dad out in the ocean? For the sharks to eat?"

"I am afraid your brother is right," Alfredo said. "But you do not have to put him in with the sharks. Not too far offshore there is a great river in the sea—the Gulf Stream—it will carry your father north for a thousand miles."

"The Gulf Stream?"

"Yeah, Sandy! The ocean will take Dad away."

"Yes, you must bring your father to this river in the sea and let him go in its powerful current."

"But how will we know where it is?" I asked. "It's all just water out there, isn't it?"

"Oh, no," Alfredo explained, "it is not all just water. First, there is the shelf of land that stretches underwater from the beach outward. The water over the shelf is green. Then there is the reef, where the water begins to turn bright blue. And just beyond the reef, you will find the Gulf Stream. It is unmistakable. The water of the Gulf Stream is blue-black, and it flows northward. You will see the change of color and feel the powerful pull of current."

Alfredo asked Jack to hand him a rolled-up chart that was on his desk, and pressed it flat on his knees.

"You see this water between Florida and Cuba? That is where the Gulf Stream snakes through. Boat captains know they are close to it when they see the frigate birds. These big black birds soar out over the Stream and dive for its many fish. It is quite a voyage in a small boat, but one you boys must make. The skiff's little engine will get you there and back, and the freedom boat will float well over the waves. It has already made it across the Gulf Stream once. With no one to row it, the boat will drift with the current, until . . ."

"Until what?" I said.

"Until the canvas becomes waterlogged and the boat sinks," Alfredo said, "or until someone finds it out at sea. In any case, what happens to your father at sea will be out of your hands."

"I hope he floats forever," Jack said.

"Me too," I said.

Alfredo rolled up the map and placed it on his bunk.

"Go out beyond the reef and look for the big black birds. Head for the birds and you will find the Stream. Then cut your father loose in it."

"Can you come with us?" I asked, but I knew Alfredo couldn't.

"He's hurting," Jack said, "and we gotta do this *now*. If we get caught with a dead body, all kinds of people will be on us."

"You can't go now!" Alfredo said. "It is already seven o'clock. There will be too many boats on the water, heading out to the reef to fish and dive all day."

He tried to stand again, this time making it to his feet. Looking out the window at the *Libertad* with the patchwork mummy inside, he said, "To-morrow morning, early. He will keep until then. But go outside now and cover your father with one of the tarps you find on the deck. Watch for snakes. They like to hide under such things."

Jack did as Alfredo said while I cooked a breakfast of eggs and bacon. The bacon smell drew Alfredo away from his bunk and over to the table, where he slid into the booth seat next to the iguana. Jack came back in sniffing and licking his lips to taste the greasy-smoke-flavored air sticking to them. We were starving.

"I covered the *Libertad* with a big tarp but I didn't tuck it all around Dad like we did the sail. You can't tell that it's a body now."

"Bueno!" Alfredo said, holding his hands in a prayer of thanks before eating.

The food tasted incredible! Jack asked Alfredo if we could fry up some more and the second batch of eggs and bacon tasted even better. The experience of the night before had heightened our senses. Being in the presence of death seemed to make us feel more alive. Even our taste buds were affected.

Suddenly Alfredo put his fork down and said, "Listen!"

The sound of a powerboat roared closer and closer and soon was idling right outside. We heard the boat bang against the ladder. The engine stopped.

"Who could that be?" I whispered.

"We may be too late," Alfredo said. "Let me do all the talking."

We heard a person climb the ladder and walk across the deck. I thought I heard the breathless sound someone makes when they are startled. Then the door began to open but the person wouldn't step inside.

"Sandy? Jack? Mr. Sanchez? Is anyone in there?"

"Mia!" I called out.

"Mia?" Alfredo was confused.

Mia pushed the door open all the way and walked in.

"I think I just saw a snake!" she said.

"You probably did," Jack told her.

"What are you doing here, Miss Petruzzo?" Alfredo asked.

"I came to warn you! This morning in the restaurant I heard someone from Paradise Isle

Marina say that some guy rented a boat yesterday and never brought it back. They're looking for the boat and the guy. He said the customer had sandy-colored hair and walked with a limp. I knew it was your father but I didn't say anything. You have to get out of here! He's probably somewhere around here right now."

"He already found us," Jack said.

"He did?"

"Yeah," I said. "He found us yesterday." I started to tell Mia what had happened, but Alfredo stopped me.

"Are you sure Mia should be told this? You boys have to be very careful." He turned to Mia. "Did anybody come with you?"

"No," Mia told him. "I came alone in my parents' ski boat. I have to get it back soon or they'll start asking questions. I've known Sandy and Jack's secret and I've kept it. You don't have to worry about me."

"Yeah, Alfredo," Jack said. "Mia's a pirate too!"

"She is?" Alfredo said. "Then I will trust her as you do."

We told Mia about what happened with Dad. She had to sit down and when she did, she sat right on the iguana. They both were frightened. Mia nearly hit the ceiling. Jack thought it was hilarious and his laughter lightened the mood in the room.

"Now we gotta bring him out to the ocean and set him free in the Gulf Stream," I said to Mia after she had calmed down.

"The Gulf Stream?"

"Yes," Alfredo told her. "The boys have to dispose of their father's body without being discovered. The Stream will carry him away. I wish I could help, but I cannot move very well right now. And it has to be done soon."

"He's here?"

"Yeah," Jack answered. "Outside in the freedom boat."

Mia rushed to the cabin door and looked down at the *Libertad*.

"Under the tarp?"

"Yes," Alfredo said, "they will be towing him with my skiff."

Mia kept staring down at the tarp-covered boat. "I can take them!" she said. "I know about the Gulf Stream. Daddy takes us fishing out there. We can go in a small boat. Lots of people do. There hasn't been much wind. The water will be calm most of the way. I know a canal not far from here. We can take that out to the ocean."

"Yes," Alfredo said. "I know that canal. This is a good plan. You may need to bring an extra can of gas. There's a full one out on deck."

"We should leave early tomorrow morning, before daylight," Mia said, "so we can get away from shore before many other boats are out."

"Yes! Yes!" agreed Alfredo. "This is a good ally you have!" he said to me.

"Three o'clock!" Jack decided for us.

"Three. I'll pick you up at the restaurant dock at three in the morning," I told Mia.

I walked Mia out on deck and as we passed a

pile of old life preservers, she grabbed my hand.

"That's where I saw something that moved like a snake!" she said.

She held my hand all the way to the ladder and when she turned to climb down, she let my hand go. The *Libertad* was to her left and she looked at the tarp as she stepped down the ladder to her boat. I worried she might change her mind.

"See you at three," I said.

Mia nodded and started the big inboard engine. Then she shoved herself off and powered away. The girl amazed me! I couldn't figure her out. I knew that the trip out to the Gulf Stream would not be as scary with her along.

We spent the rest of the day listening to Alfredo's stories about the great Gulf Stream. He said the biggest fish in the ocean live there—swordfish and sailfish, giant marlin, huge yellowfin tuna and sharks—feeding in the powerful current on vast schools of mackerel. He himself had caught a marlin measuring more than ten feet long. Alfredo showed us the long black bill of his marlin. Jack held it, touching the pointed tip again and again with the palm of his hand.

Alfredo went over the map with us again to be sure we understood where we were going and what we were in for. I could tell he was concerned for our safety.

"Once you get your father to the blue-black water, cut him loose quickly," Alfredo emphasized, "before the powerful current takes you too far."

That night, Jack and I lay down in a corner of the cabin on some pillows and blankets Alfredo bunched up for us. Neither of us could sleep thinking about the great blue-black river in the sea into which we would be taking Dad.

CHAPTER **14**

REQUIEM

It must have been around one o'clock in the morning when something inside me told me it was time to go. I roused Jack, who had just barely dozed off. Alfredo was snoring away on his bunk. We left noiselessly to make the long, slow trip with Dad in tow to pick up Mia.

Jack sat in the front of the skiff and held the flashlight while I motored slowly down the long channel, following only Jack's beam of light.

When we reached the open water of the bay, it was harder to tell which direction to go. Everything on the dark shore looked the same. Finally I recognized the silhouette of the Petruzzos' restaurant deck and aimed for the shape.

In order not to whack the prop in the very shallow water, we rowed the last fifty feet or so to shore, nudging the skiff onto the beach so Mia could enter at the bow without getting her shoes wet. The *Libertad* was out on its tow line, floating in about a foot of water.

"I brought a thermos full of cold water," she said as she climbed aboard. "There's no shade out on the ocean. We'll need something to drink."

She was wearing a red bandana tied tight around her head and big hoop earrings.

"You look like a pirate now!" Jack said.

"Yes. I guess I do." Mia smiled.

Then Jack and I poled us back out until we were in deep enough water for me to lower the prop and start the engine. I motored very slowly, feeling the tug of the tow line as we headed back toward the channel. The prop nicked bottom a few times.

"It's hard to see the shallow water in the dark," I said to Mia.

"Just keep your bow pointed toward that blinking light. It's the Kmart traffic light. Daddy taught me it'll keep you in a trough of deep water all the way to the channel. That's what I do, even during the daytime."

I aimed the skiff at the blinking light and held that course. We didn't hit bottom again.

I wanted to know more about this girl who knew how to drive a boat and navigate through shallow bays, and who was willing to take the risk she was by helping us with Dad.

"Why are you helping us? Aren't you afraid of getting in trouble?" I asked.

"Whaddaya talking about, Sandy?" Jack interrupted. "She's helping us 'cause we need help. She's a pirate just like Alfredo, and pirates help pirates!"

"Well, first of all," Mia said, "I'm helping you

because I like you. You've had some bad things happen to you. I guess I figure that once we get your dad to the Gulf Stream and cut him loose, most of your trouble will float away with him." She turned to Jack. "As for me being a pirate? Everybody in the Keys has a little pirate in them!"

Jack and Mia laughed together. I just stared at Mia.

I steered into the channel. It didn't seem like night anymore. My eyes were getting used to the dark. I could see the water ahead clearly.

Mia found the narrow man-made canal that would lead us through the mangroves to the ocean.

"There!" She pointed and I turned, forgetting we were towing a boat. We heard the *Libertad* bump hard against the canal wall as it made the turn too sharply behind us. Jack shone the flashlight on it.

"It's okay," he said.

The canal that cut through Key Largo to the

ocean was much narrower than the channel. Jack shone the light to our left, then to our right, to help me keep in the center. When Jack's light flashed on a great big waterside bush covered with red flowers, Mia asked me to slow down and steer closer so she could pick some as we passed. She dropped big red flowers one by one into the skiff. When she had a pile of them in the center of the skiff, she motioned me to go on. Jack shone the light on the pile.

"Hibiscus," Mia said. "They're my favorite! And they'll make beautiful funeral flowers for your father."

We finally came to the end of the canal and saw the ocean side of Key Largo. Up until this time, we had only seen the bay side, which was dotted with mangrove islands. The ocean side was something else—a great expanse of water as far as the eye could see. The sun wasn't up yet, but the sky looked bright.

"It's huge!" Jack said.

"Is this the first time you've ever seen the ocean?" Mia asked.

"Yeah," I told her. "We've seen it on TV but never thought it'd be like this—so big."

"It sure is," Mia said.

I let up on the throttle and slowed down to try and get used to the sight. But the longer I looked, the less used to it I felt, and the less I wanted to head out in it.

"You're gonna have to go faster, Sandy, if you want to keep your tow line tight," Mia said.

I looked behind us and saw the tow line bobbing and bouncing on the water. I gave the engine more gas and the line lifted and tightened, pulling the *Libertad* through the water again.

"The reef is straight ahead about four miles," Mia said. "The Gulf Stream will be out beyond the reef."

Jack crawled from his seat in the bow and sat next to Mia in the center of the skiff. He took her arm in his hand, pulled the black marker from his pocket and began drawing the croc skull and crossed bones on her skin. Mia looked down, watching Jack draw. He added the croc teeth and darkened the eyes and shaded under the crossed bones.

"Now," he said, patting Mia on the shoulder as if he were making her a knight, "you're one of us. You're one of the Pirates of Crocodile Swamp!"

"I love it!" Mia exclaimed, turning her arm to admire Jack's work. "Jack, you're quite an artist!"

Jack's face turned beet red.

I spotted a big sea turtle floating, but before I could point it out to Mia and Jack, the turtle went under, slapping the surface with its flippers. Waves began hitting the skiff's bow and the ride got a little bumpy. Three fish shot out of a wave into the air.

"Flying fish!" Mia shouted, as one of them plopped into our boat. It had fins like other fish, but the fins on its sides, near its gills, were extra long. Mia scooped the fish out of the boat and threw it high and the fish glided on its long fin-wings back into the waves.

"Cool!" Jack said. He crawled forward and sat on the bow to watch for more flying fish.

"Have you ever been across the ocean?" I asked Mia.

"No," she said, "but I know what's out there. Daddy told me."

"What's out there?" Jack asked.

Mia straightened up in her seat and pointed. "North and east, it goes to the islands of the Bahamas. They're only about sixty miles away, I think." She turned in her seat and pointed again. "South and east, it goes to Cuba. Cuba is one hundred miles away. And beyond those places, it goes all the way to Africa."

"Let's go to Africa!" Jungle Jack called out from his perch in the bow.

"Uh—I don't think so!" I said. "Unless you want to steer the skiff all that way."

By the time we had slowly towed the *Libertad* as far as the reef, the sun was up and shining brightly. Mia opened the thermos and poured some water into three little plastic cups she had also brought.

"Come on, guys, drink!" she said. "The sun's hot on us now. We need to drink some water."

I slowed down so we could look over the side into the clear water and see the colorful coral. They looked close enough to touch, close enough to hit our prop. Mia must have read my mind.

"There's always plenty of water over the reef for small boats to pass," she said.

Jack pointed to a big, brown, branchy coral. "That looks like a deer's antlers," he said.

"That's called staghorn coral," Mia told him. She reached her hand into the water and pointed around. "The ones that look like waving fans are fan corals. That one that has all the star shapes on it is a star coral."

A large barracuda dashed out from under the skiff and Mia quickly pulled her hand from the water.

"I should have known better," she said, pulling the rings off her fingers. "Barracuda are attracted to the sparkle and flash of jewelry. That's how people get bit." She put her hand back in the water to point again.

"That big round coral that looks like a giant brain is . . ."

"Let me guess," I said. "That's a brain coral."

Mia winked at me. "You got it!"

The barracuda swam up again, this time just to eyeball our boat and us in it. It had a long snout and long jagged teeth.

"Wow!" Jack said. "That's a mean-looking fish!" Then he said, "Look, a nurse shark!"

Down below the barracuda, between two coral mounds, a big brown shark was moving slowly over the sand. We all watched the shark cruise along the bottom.

"Do you know why they call those sharks nurse sharks?" Mia asked us.

"I bet Jungle Jack knows," I said. Mia and I looked at him.

"I don't know," Jack admitted. "I thought it was just a name."

"They call them nurse sharks because they rarely leave the area they were born in," Mia explained. "They spend their whole lives in their 'nursery.'"

A large school of yellow minnows swam by, followed by a sea turtle flapping its flippers like it was flying underwater. The skiff was moving just fast enough for us to see the reef and still tow the *Libertad* over the gentle swells. On the far side of the reef, Jack spotted two spiny lobsters walking one behind the other. Then the bottom dropped so deeply, we couldn't see anything but water.

Right there, the color of the ocean changed from green to bright blue, just like Alfredo said it would. Higher waves started hitting the boat. I goosed the gas to get us going faster through them. Then I throttled up to full speed and the skiff plowed through, sending a spray over the bow with every wave.

"Are we getting close?" I asked Mia.

"Look!" Jack yelled. "Alfredo's big birds!"

Ahead, three huge black birds with long swallow-like tails were circling in the sky.

"That's it! The Gulf Stream!" Mia said.

I stretched tall in my seat to look. Then I stood, still steering, to see better.

"Looks like somebody spilled a great big bottle of black ink into the blue water," I said.

"It's true," Mia said. "Look how dark the water is."

A huge fish shot up out of the blue-black waves.

"Sailfish!" Mia yelled. "That's the kind Daddy comes out here to catch!"

The big fish sailed through the air, shaking its long pointed bill, then it splashed back down near a floating mass of weeds that Mia called sargassum. Patches of the yellow sargassum weeds were floating all around the surface, as far as we could see, but none were floating on the dark water of the Stream. The weed islands bumped and

bunched alongside the dark water and the changing current.

Along with the sargassum, trash from shore—
planks of wood, broken sheets of plywood, Styrofoam, lost lobster buoys, coconuts—all floated on
the edge of the great river in the sea. It was as if
the powerful northward flow of the Gulf Stream
was too fast a train to hop, and all the flotsam and
jetsam that had drifted out to sea couldn't catch a
ride.

I wasn't so sure I wanted to ride it and slowed
the skiff. But Mia urged me to keep our speed up
and power onward.

"Don't worry, Sandy. We won't sink. Just keep
your bow pointed into the waves," she told me.

I steered the skiff through the maze of floating
debris and headed into the dark water, turning
our bow into the waves. Once I had the skiff and
the *Libertad* pointed right into the strong
current, I throttled up and the skiff's engine held
us there. The waves were high but we rode them

well and the *Libertad* slid over them one after another. One of the frigate birds plunged after a fish.

"Cut Dad loose!" Jack yelled from the bow.

I handed the job of steering over to Mia and she held us against the current while I picked up the fish knife and began cutting the tow line. It was pulled tight, and was hard to cut. The bouncing boat didn't help matters. I missed the rope and cut my hand.

"Be careful!" Mia shouted.

I kept cutting the rope, sucking the blood coming out of my hand to keep it from dripping into the water and attracting the Gulf Stream sharks Alfredo told us about. Then Mia suddenly yelled, "Wait! Pull him closer!"

"Why?"

"The flowers!"

I pulled the *Libertad* close. Jack worked his way to the back of the boat and helped. Then I took the tiller as Mia stood and threw all of the big red hibiscus flowers onto Dad's body. That's when a rogue wave smashed against the side of the boat, pouring water in and nearly knocking Mia overboard. I grabbed her arm just in time.

"Cut Dad loose!" Jack yelled to me. "He's dragging us down!"

All the water in the skiff was keeping our stern low and dragging the Libertad down. The two boats tethered together were pulling each other down. We were in danger of losing Dad and sinking along with him! I chopped at the tow line. Mia and Jack began frantically scooping water out of the skiff with their cupped hands. I sliced through the rope with the sharpest portion of the knife blade and finally cut through. The rope fell and the Libertad, buoyant again, drifted away from us. Mia and Jack had gotten a lot of the water out of the skiff and we began floating higher.

I steered us into the next oncoming wave, surfing with it a little ways to get us turned safely toward the edge of the Stream and out of the dark water, back into the blue. When we were gliding on gentler waves, I let Jack steer and went forward to Mia, sitting in the center of the boat. She was sobbing quietly.

"You okay?" I asked.

"I'm okay. I just don't know what would have happened to me out there if you hadn't . . ." She couldn't finish.

"You would've climbed up on a wave and ran over it to the boat! That's what!" I said, believing she could do anything, and when Mia laughed, I felt everything from then on was going to be okay.

"Look!" Jack said.

He saw the *Libertad* riding high over a giant wave. Mia and I saw it too.

"Good-bye, Dad," I said. Mia simply closed her eyes to pray.

It was hard leaving Dad out there. I watched and watched until I could no longer see any part of the *Libertad* rising and falling on the blue-black Stream. Jack watched the water for a long time after Dad was out of sight. Tears were pouring

down his cheeks. Seeing him cry made me cry. Mia cried too.

"Bye, Dad," Jack said to himself, still looking out to sea.

Then he squeezed the throttle and raced the skiff farther and farther away from the black water. He pounded that little boat all the way back to the reef. The sun was shining brightly, and its glare on the water made it harder to see down to the coral as clearly as we could earlier.

There were other boats out over the reef. Some

were fishing. Some were full of snorkelers diving and swimming. We left them all behind us and glided on flat calm water to the inlet, through the canal, down the channel and across the bay, all the way back to the restaurant beach.

CHAPTER **15**
SPRING
1982

In the spring of 1982 we started our lives over. While back in Pennsylvania new leaves were sprouting on the hardwood trees, wildflowers were pushing up through melting snow and young new grass blades would have been just beginning to grow over Terry's small grave, Jack and I were experiencing our own new beginning, trying our best to leave all we had known and all we had been through in the past. I thought a lot about

221

Mom, but Dad's confession just before he died convinced me she was gone too. In the month and a half since Dad's death, we had moved in with Alfredo.

Living on the snake- and rat-infested tub wasn't as bad as I thought it would be, but it took some getting used to. Then one day Alfredo decided we were going to clean the old boat up, and things changed for the better.

For one whole week, all we did was clear the deck. We hauled the trash down the ladder into the skiff and took it to a Dumpster in the Paradise Isle Marina. We made more than a hundred trips! We must have taken away all the rats too, or else they jumped ship and swam to the bridge boulders, because we never saw one on the boat again after that. The snakes were something else, though. They held on. We had to be very careful whenever we picked something up. When one of us saw a snake, we would call Alfredo and he would use a long broom handle to flip the snake overboard. Once a snake got flipped, it didn't climb back up.

When we had all the trash off the deck, and the rats and snakes along with it, we got down on our hands and knees and scrubbed. Alfredo was right down there with us, scrubbing hard. His hip had stopped hurting. The old wood grain really came through and shone like new. Little One took to venturing out on the deck more, running across the beautiful wood. One particularly fast dash caused the iguana to start sliding, and it slid right off the deck. Jack rescued it with a long-handled fish net. I was surprised to see how well an iguana could swim. Alfredo told me green iguanas swim all the time in the wild.

Some crocs hunted in the area around Alfredo's boat. None of them were as big as Annabelle. We never saw her again. She stayed inside the swamp. Once in a while we'd see the hammerhead cruising around. We felt safer seeing it from the high deck. Jack actually enjoyed watching the big shark. He even asked Alfredo for some paper and a pencil so that he could draw it.

We scrubbed the cabin's outside walls, or "bulkheads" as Alfredo called them, and we painted the window frames dark green. We cleaned and painted every part of the boat except the stern, which was backed up against the mangroves.

Alfredo showed Jack how to oil all the hinges on the doors and hatches. I polished the brass. Alfredo called the brass rails and fittings and latches "brightwork."

Jack and I felt at home with Alfredo. We fished every day, sometimes from the skiff and sometimes from the deck of the big boat. Alfredo taught us special fishing knots and how to use lures instead of bait for the big snook and redfish that hid under the mangroves. The motion of the lures teased the fish until, out of curiosity or just plain anger, they swam out to take a bite. When they did, we would be reeling like crazy.

We swam and snorkeled and told stories and lived every day as if it were free for the taking. But deep down inside, Jack and I knew we weren't really free. We were still hiding. Alfredo was trying to think of a way to get us enrolled in school, perhaps under different names, so he could still keep us with him. But no one would believe we were even distantly related. It was well known that Alfredo had no relatives living in the United States. So we kept hiding out, not knowing what to do.

After school each day Mia came with leftovers from the restaurant. She was allowed to use her parents' boat, and as long as she didn't stay away too long, they didn't worry about her. Jack and I trusted Mia, but Alfredo was never completely sure about her. She was a good friend, interested only in our welfare. Mia couldn't stand that we weren't going to school. And she was frustrated by the fact that we didn't have a clue what to do about it. Alfredo worried that she would try to solve our problems on her own. So far she hadn't. Then one day Mia did something that neither Jack nor I nor Alfredo ever would have thought she would do.

It was late in the afternoon, around four or five o'clock. Jack and I were up on the cabin roof, giving it a coat of the dark green paint. Alfredo was down on the deck polishing a brass bell he had found tucked away in the cabin.

"Look, boys," he said. "Your friend Mia is coming down the channel."

She was still a mile away at least, but we could see it was Mia's boat. Only she wasn't ripping up the water the way she usually did. She was creeping down the channel, barely making waves. When she got a little closer, Jack made a groaning sound.

"She's not alone. She's got somebody with her!"

"Yes," Alfredo said, "I'm afraid so."

"How could she?" Jack shouted. "She promised she wouldn't tell anybody about us!"

"But she has," Alfredo said, watching Mia's boat approach. "*Muy malo*—very bad."

I stared at the coming boat and the person sitting tall and straight in the seat beside Mia. It was a woman, and she was dressed in a brown suit. My heart sank inside my chest. Our secret was out. Mia had ruined everything and I hated her for it. Then the woman in the boat pushed her hair back away from her face and I suddenly recognized her.

"It's Mom!" Jack screamed at the top of his lungs. "It's Mom! It's Mom! It's Mom!" he sang, as he danced all around the unpainted half of the cabin roof.

Mia and Mom heard and waved.

"Sandy! Jack!" Mom called up to us.

I couldn't believe my eyes or ears! It *was* Mom,

looking like a million bucks in a new suit and new hairdo, and smiling like an angel.

"This is your mother?" Alfredo asked me.

"Yep! That's our mom!" I said.

"Bueno! Bueno!" Alfredo shouted. He picked up the iguana at his feet and held it high, kissing the big lizard right on its scaly lips.

"Bueno! Bueno!" he said again with happy tears dripping uncontrollably from the corners of his kind old eyes. I started crying too. And Jack— he was bawling and laughing and singing all at the same time.

Mia pulled the boat beside Alfredo's and we helped Mom climb up the ladder. She hugged Jack and me together so tightly, she squeezed more tears out of us. She smelled great—like perfume and chewing gum.

"You're not dead!" Jack said over and over, burying his face in Mom's brown suit.

"No, I'm not dead. For a while I felt like I was. I lost your baby brother. I thought I lost the two of you. I was badly hurt and I was very sick, but I got well again and—"

"You're here!" Jack said.

"Yes, I'm here, honey," Mom said. "I've found you. I found you both!"

"You found us!" Jack said.

"Yes. Thanks to Mia."

Mia was standing off to the side, clutching a crumpled sheet of paper. She handed it to me. It was a MISSING notice with pictures of Jack and me on it.

"I saw it early this morning in the post office," Mia said.

"She called right away," Mom added, "and I flew right down!"

Mia's eyes started to tear up and we pulled her into the hug. Mom reached a hand to Alfredo.

"My name is Rose. Thank you for all you have done for my boys. Mia told me everything."

"It was my pleasure," Alfredo said, shaking

Mom's hand. "They have given me much more than I could ever give them."

A flock of birds, white against the deep blue sky, flew over so low we could hear their wing beats.

"They're beautiful!" Mom said, watching the birds glide down over the mangroves. "Wonder what kind they are?"

Jack and I said together, "Ibises."